He was offering Louise the chance to get rid of his lingering legacy, yes.

But not his way.

Hers.

"Your idea is a nonstarter, Giacomo. I'm not coming back to Milan with you." She gave a short laugh. "And I'm definitely not going to pretend to be your wife."

"So you are refusing?" he said, his words edged with the frustration of a man who was used to getting exactly what he wanted.

"Yes, I am refusing," she agreed, before drawing in a deep breath. "But I have an alternative idea."

The glitter of his black eyes showed his displeasure. He didn't like being thwarted, Louise remembered. He didn't like anyone else taking control or making counterproposals.

"Really?" he clipped out, tapping his middle finger against the table in a familiar gesture of irritation. "And what idea is that?"

"That I come to Barton for Christmas. But not as your wife." She paused, allowing time for her words to sink in. "As your housekeeper."

Sharon Kendrick once won a national writing competition by describing her ideal date: being flown to an exotic island by a gorgeous and powerful man. Little did she realize that she'd just wandered into her dream job! Today she writes for Harlequin, and her books feature often stubborn but always to-die-for heroes and the women who bring them to their knees. She believes that the best books are those you never want to end. Just like life...

Books by Sharon Kendrick

Harlequin Presents

Cinderella in the Sicilian's World
The Sheikh's Royal Announcement
Cinderella's Christmas Secret
One Night Before the Royal Wedding
Secrets of Cinderella's Awakening

Conveniently Wed!

His Contract Christmas Bride

The Legendary Argentinian Billionaires

Bought Bride for the Argentinian
The Argentinian's Baby of Scandal

Visit the Author Profile page
at Harlequin.com for more titles.

Sharon Kendrick

CONFESSIONS OF
HIS CHRISTMAS
HOUSEKEEPER

♦HARLEQUIN
PRESENTS

HARLEQUIN® PRESENTS®

Recycling programs
for this product may
not exist in your area.

ISBN-13: 978-1-335-56815-1

Confessions of His Christmas Housekeeper

Copyright © 2021 by Sharon Kendrick

This edition published by arrangement with Harlequin Books S.A.

For questions and comments about the quality of this book,
please contact us at CustomerService@Harlequin.com.

Harlequin Enterprises ULC
22 Adelaide St. West, 40th Floor
Toronto, Ontario M5H 4E3, Canada
www.Harlequin.com

Printed in U.S.A.

CONFESSIONS OF HIS CHRISTMAS HOUSEKEEPER

During the writing of every book comes an angst-ridden moment when I lift the phone to call Sarah Nicolson. This one's for her.

CHAPTER ONE

THERE HAD TO be some kind of mistake.

Giacomo Dante Volterra stared, unable to believe the evidence of his own eyes. He shook his head in disbelief. He was one of the richest men in Italy. He owned a plane, many homes, fabulous art and fast cars. In the past he had embraced daredevil and extreme sports. His mouth hardened. Just not any more.

Yet now he was confused as he stared at the woman who was emerging through a door leading into the office where he sat, slightly impatiently—for he did not like to be kept waiting—and rehearsed the momentous thing he was about to say to her.

But the words remained unsaid. They stuck in his throat like dust. And although these past months he had learned to live with confusion as a regular companion, this time it was off the scale.

Could this woman *really* be his wife?

His eyes narrowed, because, judging from the

sudden pallor of her face and the open-mouthed shock she made no attempt to hide, on balance he would say that, yes, she probably was—though there could be another reason for her shock, he reminded himself grimly. But the fact remained that she was not what he had been expecting to see. How could any wife of his look like *this*?

She wore a garish pink uniform, which hugged the curving outline of her petite body, and her dark hair was piled up on top of her head and covered snugly in an ugly white hairnet. She wore flat black shoes—his mouth twisted with distaste, for he had always preferred heels—and no jewellery whatsoever. Certainly not a wedding ring. He guessed he should be grateful for that. Because wouldn't that make his proposition even trickier, if she was sentimentally holding on to a brief period in her life which he had completely forgotten?

He found himself wondering why she wasn't covered from head to foot in designer clothes, dripping with diamonds and living in a fancy London apartment—while filling up the lazy hours with trips to the gym and girlie lunches. Yet his bank account showed no payments to his estranged wife, which meant she had made no claim on his fortune and was obviously supporting herself. Which was surprising because he was used to picking up the bill. It was one of the many things which were predictable when you had as much money as he did.

It seemed inexplicable that any wife of his was working for a catering firm in a small village not far from Heathrow airport. The narrow streets seemed to be competing for the dubious honour of displaying the most garish Christmas decorations he had ever seen, and there was an illuminated sleigh stuck to the front of one of the houses.

'Giacomo,' she said in a low voice, sounding as if his name were a substitute for the word 'devil'.

But he noticed the way she bit her lip, as if her question were underpinned with something else other than suspicion and faint hostility, and idly he wondered what that might be.

'What are you doing here?'

'Hello, Louise,' he said carefully, as if he were trying out a word in a new language. 'Good to see you, too.'

Louise didn't answer. She didn't dare. She couldn't think. Couldn't speak. Her head was buzzing and so were her thoughts. She had felt an unstoppable kind of excitement when she had walked in and seen him sitting there, the most beautiful and sexy man she had ever set eyes on. The man she had—unbelievably—been married to for about a nanosecond, before it all went horribly wrong. But the use of her proper name told her that this was not Giacomo turning up and telling her he'd made a terrible mistake and please could they try again. She wouldn't have wanted that anyway, would she?

Would she?

A sense of resolve rushed through her veins as she met the blackness of his eyes. No, she most certainly would not. She was better off without him because he was wrong for her on so many levels. Incapable of giving or receiving love, Giacomo Volterra had pushed her away with all the chilly force of an east wind. He had never been there for her when she had needed him most.

But she felt a sharp pang of sadness all the same, because the past always had the power to make you feel unbearably poignant. It could wrap itself around your heart with its dark tentacles and squeeze and squeeze until you felt a sharp pain. She was no longer Lulu, she recognised dully. His Lulu. She was Louise—and as soon as she could bring herself to file for divorce, her surname would be Greening again and not Volterra. And that would be a good thing. Hadn't she told herself that over and over?

Now that her initial surprise had worn off and she had composed herself a little, she allowed herself to study him more closely and that was when she got her second shock. Because suddenly she became aware of the scar zigzagging down one of his cheeks—which marred the perfection of a sculpted face which made grown women swoon. There was another small scar over his left eyebrow—one which most people probably wouldn't have noticed except that she used to spend so many hours fluttering kisses over his skin that sometimes she felt she knew him by touch alone. It was like seeing a once perfect porcelain jar which had shattered into many pieces before being pieced back together again. There was nothing wrong with the new version—it was just very different from the old one.

And then she looked into his eyes. Properly. Those intense eyes which could capture you in their dark spotlight and make you feel as if you were the only person on the planet he wanted to talk to. They could be sexy and caressing eyes, especially when he was slowly removing your clothes or easing himself deep inside you, but today she could see nothing but an emptiness in their depths—as if some vital light had been extinguished. It was, she thought, like looking into the eyes of a stranger. A stranger who was incongruously sitting beside a black and pink sign reading *Posh Catering: service with class!*

'What are you doing here?' she asked again, more calmly this time. 'And what have you done with my boss?'

'She'll be back shortly.' He sat back in his chair as if he owned the place, the harsh office lighting making his hair appear as dark as a raven's wing. 'I persuaded her to give us a few moments alone.'

She raised her eyebrows. 'She's usually chained to her desk—you must have been very persuasive.'

'I am,' he said silkily, 'nothing if not persuasive, Louise. Surely you know that? But I needed to speak to you. Alone.'

Louise felt the prickle of something which felt uncomfortably like hope because even though you knew all the reasons why someone was bad for you, it didn't seem to stop you from wanting them. It didn't stop her skin from icing into goosebumps when his strangely cold, black gaze skated over her. And that was nothing but a hormonal reaction, she told herself fiercely. It's your neglected body reminding you that here is someone capable of bringing you immeasurable pleasure.

'Well, here's your opportunity. Speak away. Though you'll have to make it brief.' She gave an entirely unnecessary glance at her wristwatch, just to illustrate the point. 'As you can see, I'm working.'

Beneath his dark cashmere overcoat, he shrugged, drawing her unwilling attention to the width and power of his shoulders, and, with an effort, Louise pushed the thought away. How was fixating on that stuff going to help her get over him, as she'd been trying to get over him since the moment she'd realised she couldn't keep fooling herself any longer?

The moment when she'd wised up and accepted that their marriage really *was* over.

'Brevity might be difficult,' he murmured. 'This isn't the kind of thing which can be conveyed in a few words.'

'That's a pity, because I really haven't got time to hear any more. Maybe write it all down, in a letter.'

She made to turn away but the extraordinary thing he said next stopped her in her tracks.

'Please.'

And Louise froze because Giacomo didn't ask like that. Not usually. He snapped his fingers or issued terse commands and, because he looked the way he did and because he could be charming and ruthless in equal measure, people just caved in and did whatever he wanted. They rolled over and smiled. Hadn't she done it herself—when she'd broken all her self-imposed rules and fallen into bed with him a few hours after their first meeting?

But the direct appeal in his voice was having an effect on her. She could feel herself wavering, despite her suspicions that whatever he wanted to say had the potential to make her feel wobbly. Because who in their right mind would run the risk of breaking down in floods of tears at their place of work? She supposed she could send him packing and tell him she had no desire to engage in *any* kind of conversation but, not only would that be immature, it would also be a bit of a giveaway. It might indicate to him that she was still vulnerable where he was concerned and she wasn't, was she?

Was she?

No. That ship had sailed. And wasn't the truth that she was curious, wondering what had brought him back into her life when he'd been happy enough to see her go?

Which was why she found herself nodding, although she attempted to keep her words bland and non-committal. 'I finish at five-thirty. I'll meet you in the pub for a coffee just before six. I can give you half an hour, no more.'

'Which pub?'

'There's only one pub in the village, Giacomo,' she informed him drily. 'This is England—not the throbbing metropolis of Milan.' She flicked a glance towards the gleaming black vehicle which hugged the kerb outside and which probably cost more than her boss earned in a year. 'I don't think you'll have much trouble finding it as you roar down the main street in your fancy car, but try not to break the speed limit and get yourself a ticket. Our local policeman takes his job very seriously. And now if you'll excuse me—I have two dozen pastry shells which need filling.'

She didn't turn back, not even when she heard the door close behind him, because she didn't want to watch him leave as she had done so many times before. She was actually shaking as she went back into the small industrial kitchen at the back of the shop, shrugging off her colleague's solicitous question about why she was looking so pale and whether she was ill.

'No, I'm fine,' she said, forcing a smile.

She wasn't, of course. Her hands were shaking so much that she slopped onion marmalade on the counter and nearly dropped a dish of grated cheese. She hadn't seen Giacomo in nearly eighteen months, when their marriage had imploded soon after she'd lost their baby. Furiously, she blinked her tears, making the rows of tartlets in front of her blur. Why fool herself? It would have imploded anyway. It was doomed from the beginning. They were mismatched. Her last contact with him had been during a terse international phone call when she'd told him that she wouldn't be coming back and he had ended the call without another word and blocked her number.

He'd been hospitalised in Switzerland since then of course, after a skiing accident, and Louise had been surprised by just how stricken she had been on receiving the news that he'd been badly injured. Clamping down her instinct to rush to his side, she had lifted the phone to his aide to convey her hopes and prayers for his recovery and had asked whether there was anything she could do. But the response she had received had been like a knife to the chest. Paolo had gently told her that the private clinic had been besieged by hordes of females eager to provide plenty of tender loving care for the stricken patient. The aide she'd always got on so well with had seemed eager to get her off the phone. She'd supposed that had been his way of politely telling her that Giacomo had moved on and didn't want to be bothered by her or memories of their marriage—which was possibly the only episode of failure in his star-touched and glittering existence. She had guessed he wanted to wipe her from his life, the way her teachers at school used to clean the writing from the whiteboard at the end of the day.

So why had he turned up like this, without any kind of warning, asking to see her?

She finished cooking, cleaned off the work surfaces and went to the cloakroom to remove her uniform, but as she wriggled into a pair of jeans and pulled on a sweater she could think of only one reason why he was here and she was going to need all her inner strength if her hunch proved to be true. Had he met someone else and needed a super-quick divorce so he was free to marry again? Someone he thought he was in love with this time? Someone rich and well connected like him—not an ordinary Englishwoman he'd only wed because she'd fallen pregnant after what was only ever supposed to be a few casual hook-ups.

Angrily, Louise tugged off the hairnet so that her hair tumbled around her shoulders and she ran her fingers through it to impose some sort of order on the silky mass. It shouldn't still hurt and she must be sure not to show him that it did. She would be calm when he told her. She would maintain her dignity. She would wish him every happiness, in a very grown-up kind of way. They might even engage in a little stilted conversation over a cup of coffee— which inevitably he would compare unfavourably to the brew served in his native Milan.

How are you? he would question, with the slightly patronising attitude of the ex-partner who had moved on faster than the other.

And she would say, *Me?* Perhaps she would pause to magic up a smile from somewhere and try to force a little conviction into her response. *Oh, I'm fine, thanks, Giacomo. You know. Just plodding along.*

But the imagined conversation quickly ran out of steam and Louise knew she needed to rethink her delivery. *Plodding along?* Did she really want to come over to her estranged husband sounding like a superannuated carthorse?

She brushed her hair, tied it back into a thick braid and pulled on her trusty fur-trimmed anorak before stepping out into the icy December air which stung her cheeks. The night was clear and emerging stars were visible in the indigo sky as she made her way towards the pub, her boots clipping over pavements already glittering with a diamond dusting of frost. Outside the Black Duck she could see a jolly life-size Santa swaying slightly in the breeze and there were fairy lights draped around every window of the pub. With just a few days to go until Christmas, the build-up of excitement and expectation in the little village was almost palpable and Louise steeled herself as she pushed open the door, because Christmas could be uncomfortably nostalgic at the best of times. She must be prepared to listen to corny seasonal songs, which would inevitably tug at her heartstrings, and not react to them. In fact, she must not show any emotion no matter what he had to say, because Giacomo didn't engage with emotion.

He never had.

She noticed him as soon as she stepped inside, but then so had everyone else. He was sitting beside a roaring log fire beneath a cascade of glittering golden tinsel, and she saw most people in the pub casting surreptitious looks in his direction, although some of the younger women were openly drooling. Mostly, people were behaving as if they'd never seen anyone quite like him in their midst and in that, they were right. Because men like Giacomo Volterra were rare enough in any setting, but practically unique in a small English village like this.

He had removed his overcoat to reveal his muscular body and it was proving to be a huge distraction. Clad in a pale silk shirt, worn with a pair of faded jeans which hugged his long and powerful legs, he managed to look supremely wealthy yet supremely casual. His black hair was a little longer than the close-cropped style she remembered and his angled jaw was shadowed with the virile hint of new beard. With those cold ebony eyes, which didn't miss a thing, he looked like a blazing star who had fallen into the centre of this cosy little place. He outshone all the winking rainbow lights on the Christmas tree. He made every man in the place seem like only half a man. An empty coffee cup sat on the table before him and he stood up as she approached.

'So you came,' he said softly, his velvety voice edged with steel.

'What would you have done if I hadn't?'

His eyes gleamed as he acknowledged the challenge in her voice. 'I would have come and found you and got you to change your mind.'

'And how would you have done that?'

He shrugged. 'By using my powers of persuasion, which—as you have already acknowledged—are considerable, *cara*.'

She wanted to tell him not to call her that, because she wasn't his darling any more. It reminded her too much of things he'd murmured to her when he was deep inside her body. But words were easy to say, she reminded herself bitterly. You didn't have to mean them. Much better to ignore his silken boast than to react to it, because that might give him a hint that he was still capable of getting underneath her skin. She gave him a bland smile and looked at him questioningly. 'So?'

'Coffee?' he murmured.

'Please.' She slithered out of her coat and sat as far away from his seat as possible, but she couldn't prevent her eyes from drinking him in as he went to the bar. She tried to be objective but the feelings which were coursing through her were far from objective. Suddenly she was struck by just how *emotional* she felt as she watched him say something which made the landlady laugh because this, after all, was the man she had thought she would spend the rest of her life with. Of course she had. Nobody ever exchanged wedding vows thinking that it wouldn't last.

But when she thought about it now—just over two years down the line—she realised how naïve she had been. Because she had never really known him, had she? He had made sure of that. Giacomo Volterra had always kept her at arm's length—as if by giving away anything of himself, he would be handing her too much power, and he liked to keep that all to himself.

He returned a few minutes later, bearing two cups of macchiato, and Louise took a sip and licked the froth away from her lips, before looking at him. 'Would you like to get your critique of the coffee over and done with?'

'No critique necessary. I was surprised. It's very good.' He dropped a cube of sugar into his and stirred it, returning her mocking smile with one of his own. 'England seems to have caught up with the rest of the world. Finally.'

'I'm sure the landlady of the Duck would be overjoyed to receive praise from such a discerning palate. Be sure to put a review up on the Internet.' Louise put her cup down and clasped her hands together to stop them from shaking. 'But you haven't come all the way here to talk about the coffee, have you, Giacomo?'

'No.'

'What is it, then? You want…' Make it easy for him, she urged herself. And by doing that you will make it easier for yourself, too. Take control. It's easy once you try. 'You want…' She sucked in a deep breath and tried again. 'You want to get married again?'

'I want to get married again?' he echoed, and then frowned. 'Whatever gave you that idea?'

'I just assumed—'

He gave a bitter laugh. 'Assumption is never advisable, Louise. Especially in my case. But no, not me. Not marriage. Once bitten, twice shy—as I believe you say over here.'

Louise was appalled at the relief which flooded over her, which quickly gave way to a sinking despair. His private life is none of your business, she told herself fiercely. But there was something else which was and there was no excuse for not having mentioned it before. She really ought to make some reference to his crash on the slope of one of Europe's most notorious mountains. She mustn't allow herself to be distracted by the fact that her breasts were prickling beneath her sweater as she imagined his fingers massaging them into rocky peaks. 'I was very sorry to hear about your accident.'

His eyes narrowed and his mouth twisted into a line which was almost brutal. 'Ah, my accident. I wondered when you'd get around to that. Does my face repel you, Louise?' he asked softly. 'Is that why you looked so horrified when you walked in and saw me earlier?'

Louise stared at him. He was so far off the mark it was almost laughable. She wondered how he would respond if she told him that her primary reaction to his disfigurement was one of anger and protectiveness. That she *hated* the thought of something slicing through his silken flesh, causing him pain. *Nothing about you repels me,* she wanted to say. But, of course, she didn't.

'Judging from the reaction you're getting in here, I would say that, if anything, it has only enhanced your sex appeal. It gives you a distinct air of danger, which some women find so attractive.'

'And does that include you, I wonder?'

'My views are both irrelevant and inappropriate—especially on the subject of your sex appeal.' She wondered if his ego was in need of a swift massage and if that was why he'd asked the question. Did he want her to say that, yes, she still found him hugely attractive and it was a pity they couldn't go upstairs to one of the pub's rooms which overlooked the high street, so he could rip off her panties and ride her to sweet fulfilment? Because wasn't there a part of her which wanted that? The weak, physical part of her which wasn't the side she needed him to see. Which was why she kept her face deadpan. 'What we had is firmly in the past. I'm just glad to see you're fully recovered.'

'Well, not quite,' he contradicted slowly and Louise went very still as she met an expression on his face which she couldn't quite work out, because she'd never seen it before.

'You have some lasting damage?' she questioned, aware that she was finding it difficult to speak through the lump which had suddenly risen in her throat.

'Some damage, *sì*. As to whether or not it is lasting, *no lo so*. I don't know,' he added, as if he had forgotten he was speaking in Italian. 'But that is why I am here today, Louise—because I think you can help me.'

'Me?' Underneath the table, Louise clasped her fingers together. 'How? How can I possibly help you, Giacomo?'

He lowered his voice as if he didn't want anyone to overhear and it was only later that Louise realised he probably didn't.

'Because I have lost my memory. Not all of it, but some,' he told her quietly. 'I have what the doctors call partial amnesia. It is not life-threatening—it is not necessarily permanent, but—'

'But?'

'It is infuriating. Like a blank page in an otherwise full notebook. It is a roadblock in my memory and I don't want to spend the rest of my life skirting round it. Nobody knows about it—except for my aide—and I want it to stay that way. On every other level I am operating normally and business is booming as never before.' His face darkened. 'But if any of my competitors should suspect that there is a chink in my armour, then inevitably they will capitalise on it and perhaps try to exploit it.'

'Isn't that a rather cynical view of the world, Giacomo?'

He flicked her a dismissive gaze. 'You are not a businesswoman, Louise. You have no idea how these things work.'

'Thanks for the vote of confidence,' she said drily. 'And for reminding me what it's like to be patronised by a man.'

'I did not mean to patronise you,' he said softly. 'Forgive me, if I have expressed myself too bluntly.'

It was probably those words—which came closer to an apology than anything Louise had ever received from him—which made her unlink her fingers and place them on the top of the scratched pub table, as if to anchor herself. 'I don't understand why you're telling me all this,' she said. 'We're separated. What does it have to do with me?'

'It has everything to do with you,' he grated and now she could hear raw passion in his voice. 'Because you are the missing link. The person who occupied most of the year which has been wiped from my mind, like a hard drive erased from a computer. Sometimes I glimpse a fragment of my past, but I cannot catch it. It is as though that part of my life has been torn into tiny pieces and scattered on the wind—and I want you to help me put those pieces back together. I want you to help me remember, Louise.'

CHAPTER TWO

LOUISE STARED AT her estranged husband, aware that someone had started playing a Christmas song about mistletoe and wine and a couple of women were jigging around to it. Vaguely she could hear glasses chinking and hear people raucously joining in with the corny chorus, but all she could think about was Giacomo's bizarre proposition as she sat opposite him in the village pub.

'How on earth can I help you remember?' she demanded, her voice a little unsteady. 'We hardly knew one another, not the way most couples do. Our marriage lasted barely eight months, and for most of those you were out of the country "working". Well…' She shrugged her shoulders. 'Allegedly.'

His face grew tight, as if he resented the implication behind her words, but she saw the precise moment when he decided not to pursue it, leaning forward with an expression in his coal-black eyes which she *did* recognise. For this was Giacomo when he wanted something and if she wasn't careful he would end up getting it, whether she liked it or not.

'Yes, I understand that our marriage was brief,' he said. 'But it was a big life event of which I have no recollection. And I want it. I want to remember.'

'We can't always get what we want, Giacomo. I believe someone once wrote a song about it.'

And in spite of the bizarre situation in which he found himself, Giacomo felt his lips curve into the flicker of a smile. Had she always had this sense of irreverent defiance, he wondered, and was that one of the things which had attracted him to her? He sat back in his chair and watched as she examined her fingernails, though he sensed she wasn't really seeing them. The silence between them grew and he was tempted to break it and to seek an instant answer to his question, because he liked instant results. But he was a highly skilled negotiator and sensed that now was the time to allow her to think about what he had said, and to process it. In the meantime, he sipped his coffee and allowed his gaze to drift over her with unhurried scrutiny.

His doctors had advised that information overload could be counterproductive and so he had set about learning only the most basic and important facts about the missing year. His aide had informed him that he had been married to this woman and he had the documentation to record the event, as well as a brief letter he'd discovered screwed up in the back of his desk, telling him tersely that she was leaving. He admitted to having been surprised by that, because no woman had ever walked out on him before—in fact, he usually had trouble getting rid of them. But hot on the heels of that surprise had come the flicker of something dark. Something he didn't recognise—but it had disappeared so quickly he might have simply imagined it.

He frowned. It was a mystery, particularly as there were no photos of any such wedding. The only photos he had been able to find of himself with women had come, inevitably, from the Internet. Snatched photos of a younger version of himself, taken outside famous hotels and red-carpet events in Cannes. The paparazzi had obviously gate-crashed many of his holidays, where there was invariably a scantily clad woman on his arm, nuzzling up close to him against backdrops of turquoise sea. He seemed to have a penchant for Scandinavian supermodels—stunning, rangy females who were almost tall enough to match his own six feet three. But this woman had not featured in any of those photos and did not match that template at all. She was rounded and dark and barely came up to his shoulders.

His frown deepened. Nevertheless, there was something very fresh and arresting about her, though that might have had something to do with the fact that she dressed like a student. She wore no make-up—which was rare in his experience—and her sweater had clearly been chosen for warmth rather than decoration. But although she was wholesome, there was something provocatively sensual about her which seemed to transcend all her shortcomings. Her body was curvy, her dark hair was glossy and her pale skin was almost translucent.

As for her eyes...

A fragment of recall whispered across the clouds in his mind. They were the most extraordinary eyes he had ever seen. The bleached blue colour of faded denim and fringed by startlingly dark lashes. A natural beauty, he thought suddenly. A pulse started to hammer at his temple and he could feel the sudden heat of his blood as his hungry body was stirred into life. Perhaps it was not, after all, so bizarre that he should have married such a woman.

She looked up at him. 'No,' she said.

His eyes narrowed, for he had been distracted. 'No?'

'I can't do it, Giacomo,' she said suddenly. She shook her head. 'I don't think you should even be asking me.'

'Why not?'

'Because it's not appropriate!'

'You seem to be very concerned with what is appropriate and what is not. What exactly is your objection?'

Louise stared at him. She remembered him as being cold and emotionless most of the time—not in bed, of course—but surely he wasn't so dense that he expected her to help him out as if they were old buddies? It didn't help that she still found him devastatingly sexy. Or that erotic flashbacks were hovering in the back of her mind, threatening to derail her thoughts.

'Let's think about this carefully,' she said. 'We are separated, and married couples don't go their separate ways without good reason. Yet you really expect me to take a trip down memory lane with you, in order to kick-start your memory? What exactly did you have in mind—dinner here in the village, trying to negotiate an emotional minefield over a prawn cocktail?'

'No. A single dinner will not be long enough.'

'Then what?' She raised her eyebrows. 'Several excruciatingly difficult meetings with each other at the most stressful time of the year? Do me a favour!'

'No, that's not what I'm suggesting,' he said.

'It's nearly Christmas, in case you hadn't noticed,' she continued, jerking a thumb in the direction of the flashing fir tree in the corner of the pub in case he had missed the visual clues.

'Exactly. Which is why I am here.' His gaze ran

over her with narrow-eyed scrutiny. 'You know that I have a place in the English countryside?'

Louise blinked at him in astonishment. *Of course* she knew he had a place there. His exquisite thirteenth-century estate in the glorious Chiltern hills had been where he'd taken her not long after their marriage! It had been the golden time in their relationship, when they had been happy together. Or, so she had thought.

Somehow, she remained calm. 'Yes, of course I know that. Why?'

'Then perhaps you are also aware that I'm no fan of Christmas and prefer to spend it in the relative peace of the English countryside, with nothing other than a skeleton staff to look after me. I have not been to Barton for two years—not since before my accident—and it seems inadvisable to hold on to such a large estate unless I actually use it from time to time, or so my financial advisor tells me. Which is why I am here.'

'Fascinating though your property portfolio is, Giacomo, I don't really see what any of this has to do with me.'

His eyes narrowed, as if her continuing opposition was surprising to him. 'I have several appointments here in London which require my attention and, after Christmas, I shall be returning to Milan.

I would like you to accompany me there.' He paused. 'As my wife.'

Louise stared at him, her throat growing so dry that she could hardly croak her next words out. 'Run that past me again.'

'You heard me perfectly well, Louise.'

'As your *wife*? Is this…?' She tried again. 'Is this some clumsy attempt at reconciliation, Giacomo— or just a bad attempt at a joke?'

His smile became hard and determined. She remembered that smile of old.

'It is neither of those things. Perhaps I phrased it badly,' he continued silkily. 'I want you there as my wife in name only. My quasi wife, if you like. We will share our old marital home and be seen together in public. To the outside world we will appear to be giving our marriage another go.'

She stilled. 'But we won't really be doing that?'

'We will not,' he agreed emphatically. 'But it could prove to be a useful, three-pronged exercise—'

'Wow, Giacomo—you're making it sound like a military campaign,' she said faintly, aware of the stupid hurt and disappointment which flooded through her as she listened to his emotionless words.

'There are several things I am hoping it will achieve,' he continued, unperturbed by her interjection. 'Most importantly, the return of my memory. But it will also serve as a useful distraction to anyone who suspects I have been suffering from amnesia, because there is a high level of interest in me and my affairs,' he continued. 'There always has been.'

'Isn't that a rather arrogant supposition?' she suggested.

'Not really.' He shrugged. 'It comes with the territory when you achieve billionaire status, I'm afraid. But I am told that romantic reconciliations excite a good deal of interest and can divert attention. Not only that, but too many women have been pursuing me since I recovered my health. Perhaps they falsely think I am in need of someone to look after me.' He slanted her a wolfish smile. 'A fake marriage could be just the thing to discourage them.'

Louise felt a shaft of unwanted jealousy, unable to stop herself from imagining all the beautiful women vying for his attention. His callous disregard for her feelings was breathtaking, but surely that only reinforced her certainty that she was better off without him. 'And what's in all this for me?' she questioned, somehow managing to keep her voice steady. 'You don't think I might find such subterfuge…difficult, or emotionally painful?'

His eyes narrowed and suddenly his black gaze was icy-cold again. 'You were the one who walked out on the marriage, Louise. So presumably that was exactly what you wanted. As for what's in it for you.'

He shrugged. 'You have my assurance that I will facilitate a quick divorce after you return home.'

'A divorce?' she verified. 'Let me be clear. You want me to pretend to be your wife, and you're offering me a divorce in return?'

'I am.' His lips curved into a ruthless smile. 'You want one, don't you? I'm surprised you haven't got round to instigating it before.'

She gave a lame smile. No need to tell him that she hadn't been able to face going to see a lawyer. That the financial as well as the emotional implications of such a move had been enough to make her bury her head in the sand. 'I've been busy.'

'With work?'

'That's right.' She stared at him, proud of the fact that she'd never gone running to her wealthy ex, looking for a handout. 'I have to support myself.'

'Admirable,' he breathed. 'But unnecessary. Let me be frank, Louise. I have never needed anyone but at this precise moment I need you, and I think you would be crazy to turn your back on such a favourable offer. A generous settlement at the end of our marriage could be the best present you've ever had. We live as a de facto couple for a short time and afterwards we don't ever have to see each other again. You'll be free—financially and emotionally. How does that sound?' He picked up his cup and drained the last of his coffee. 'Tempted?'

The weird thing was that Louise *was* tempted, though not for the reasons her cold husband probably imagined. Because there had always been something unfinished about her relationship with the Italian tycoon. Didn't he still occupy her thoughts way more than was probably healthy? She'd done her best to try to erase him from her mind, but she'd failed, and whenever she had tried to imagine a future without him, she had failed at that, too. It had been like running straight into a brick wall. It didn't matter how many times she told herself that such a brief relationship shouldn't merit such excessive despair, her stubborn heart refused to listen—and the reason was sitting right in front of her. Too strong and dark and sexy for his own good.

And hers.

He was offering her the chance to get rid of his lingering legacy, yes.

But not his way.

Hers.

'Your idea is a non-starter, Giacomo. I'm not coming back to Milan with you.' She gave a short laugh. 'And I'm definitely not going to pretend to be your wife.'

'So you are refusing?' he said, his words edged with the frustration of a man who was used to getting exactly what he wanted.

'Yes, I am refusing,' she agreed, before drawing in a deep breath. 'But I have an alternative idea.'

The glitter of his black eyes showed his displeasure. He didn't like being thwarted, Louise remembered. He didn't like anyone else taking control, or making counter-proposals.

'Really?' he clipped out, tapping his middle finger against the table in a familiar gesture of irritation. 'And what idea is that?'

'That I come to Barton for Christmas. But not as your wife.' She paused, allowing time for her words to sink in. 'As your housekeeper.'

His eyes narrowed. 'Are you out of your mind?'

She shrugged. 'No more than I could accuse you of being. Think about it. It needs to be a contractual arrangement and I need to know where I stand. As a housekeeper, I do—as a pretend wife, I most certainly don't. My catering background means I am perfectly qualified to take on such a role and it will certainly prevent any blurring of boundaries between us. And besides…' She paused, her gaze searching his face, dipping a tentative metaphorical toe into the water. 'You do realise I was a waitress when I met you?'

He went very still for a moment before shaking his dark head. 'I remember nothing of our relationship,' he said slowly.

It was the strangest sensation, realising that inside Giacomo's head she simply didn't exist. 'Well, I was. And maybe revisiting those roles will help jog your memory.'

His tapping finger stilled, his irritation transferring itself to his tone. 'While I can see the logic in your suggestion, you seem to forget that I already have staff in situ,' he snapped. 'I don't need a housekeeper!'

'Then improvise. Give them a few days off! Pay them double to go away and leave you alone. That's usually what you do when you have a problem, isn't it, Giacomo? You throw money at it.'

'Do I?'

'You sure do.' She hesitated. 'Whenever we had a row, you bought me a piece of jewellery.'

He frowned. 'I thought all women liked jewellery.'

'I think I would have preferred to have talked out the problem, rather than just papering over the cracks. But all that's irrelevant. Water under the bridge, as we say over here.' She glanced at her watch and rose to her feet. 'Time's up. You've had your half-hour. And you're right. It was probably a crazy idea. Forget I ever suggested it.'

'No. Wait.' He clipped out the command, the expression on his beautiful scarred face growing thoughtful. 'This is not what I envisaged, but I guess it could work,' he said slowly. 'If I were to agree, when could you start?'

Louise was just reaching for her anorak when what he was saying sank in. He had called her bluff! She met the question in his eyes. 'I can start on Wednesday,' she said slowly. 'The day before Christmas Eve.'

His eyes narrowed. 'You're not busy over Christmas?'

She wasn't going to tell him that although she had a standing invitation from her aunt, she had refused it, just as she'd done last year. She found Christmas too hard to handle. She found it hard not to think about Giacomo and the Christmas she had spent with him—and who wanted a guest who was moping around thinking about their ex?

'No. I was planning to spend it quietly at home, but I can be flexible. We can arrange it officially through Posh Catering, so it's all above board. I'll give you three days of my time, Giacomo. Take it or leave it.'

He absorbed this in silence before standing up, his powerful body towering over her, seemingly oblivious to the women in the pub who were staring at him with open lust on their faces. 'Since I have little choice, I'll take it.' He paused, his black eyes growing thoughtful. 'But won't you have a problem with your sudden change of status, Louise? Have you thought about that?'

'What status?'

He shrugged. 'Won't it be a slight fall from grace—tumbling from the position of billionaire's bride to lowly housekeeper?'

Louise clenched her fists, but, in a way, the insensitivity of his question was useful in reminding her what kind of man he really was. Didn't he realise it would be far more upsetting to be his pretend *wife*, than an honest to goodness servant? Could he really not see that? No, of course he couldn't. He only ever saw what he wanted to see. She slung her bag over her shoulder and shot him a deliberately careless look. '*You* might consider being a housekeeper a lowly position, Giacomo—but let me tell you I've always been very proud of my job!'

CHAPTER THREE

LOUISE'S MOUTH WAS dry as she drove her little car towards the vast gates of Giacomo's estate, fear and longing pulsing around her veins in equal and very confusing measures.

At least she had made it here under her own steam. Giacomo had tried sending a chauffeur-driven car for her but she had refused. She didn't want a fancy limo turning up and causing speculation among the neighbours and she didn't want anything which would drag her back into his world and make her feel she was still a part of it, because she wasn't. Her place here was only temporary and she would be a fool to forget that. More than that, she didn't want to be trapped here without the means of getting away. He had clearly been displeased by her refusal to accompany him to Italy and "pretend" to be his wife, which was probably why he'd been so dismissive when she'd asked him what she should bring to the house. Nothing, had been the answer. His permanent staff would leave the place well stocked with food and drink before their departure.

'Just make sure you arrive by midday!' had been his terse departing words.

Louise pulled a face as she passed through the ornate, wrought-iron gates because unfortunately, it was already several hours after the prescribed time.

Ahead lay the long drive leading to the amazing house where they'd spent their one and only Christmas and on either side loomed the leafless trees which dominated the rolling parkland. And over there was the lake, gleaming in the fading afternoon light, which she'd walked around as a newlywed, watching the sweet little golden-eyed ducks as they bobbed around on the water.

Stop it, she told herself fiercely. Stop romanticising the past.

Her gloved hands gripped the steering wheel but now she wished she hadn't worn them because inside her palms were hot and clammy. She was dressed warmly and sensibly and hoped she looked professional and efficient, because that was the image she wanted to convey. But inside she was churned up with a mass of conflicting emotions as she considered what she was about to do.

To any sane person, the offer her estranged husband had made her was crazy. So did that make her equally crazy to have accepted? To have told him she would be his temporary housekeeper over Christmas. To cook and serve and clean up after him— as if she had not once worn his wedding ring and been his wife. All this because he wanted to use her as a prompt for his lost memory—a bit like a stage magician's assistant holding up flash cards to give him clues. And at the end of it all, he had promised her a seamless divorce.

Oh, the romance!

Her eventual agreement had been fuelled by a gut feeling that if she *didn't* agree to his suggestion—if she turned him down—then she would spend the rest of her life regretting it. Their marriage had ended unsatisfactorily—she guessed there was no other way for a marriage *to* end—but mightn't a few days' exposure to him finally lay his ghost to rest and convince her that it had been the right thing to do? It might help *her*, as well as helping Giacomo's memory return. And she wanted that for him, though she couldn't have said why. Did it come from the same place as the fierce pain she'd felt when she had seen the scar on his face? Were the fervent vows she'd made on the day she'd married him harder to forget than she imagined?

She peered up at the sky and at the heavy clouds, which were curdling like sour milk poured into a cup of tea. The pundits were predicting snow and the bookies were taking bets on whether it was going to be a white Christmas. She sincerely hoped it wouldn't. She didn't know if she could cope with the fake romance of snow on top of everything else. With the world looking magical on the outside, while inside she and Giacomo would be circling round each other with the wariness of two natural enemies who had been stuck in a gilded cage together.

Most of all she was worried about whether she would be able to remain immune to him, because the shocking thing was how much she still fancied him. Sexual desire had been missing from her life since she'd last seen him. She had wondered if her body would ever feel anything again. Yet her stomach had turned to mush when she'd walked into the office and seen him, and she'd undergone a visceral reaction to his dark and brooding presence. Even when they'd been sitting in the pub, it had hurt to look at him and know that once he had been hers. To realise that she was still capable of being in thrall to him and all that magnetic vibrancy he exuded without even trying.

But he had never really been hers, had he? Their marriage had been born of nothing but expedience. He would have been out of her life like a shot if she hadn't been carrying his baby, and until she divorced him she would never be free.

And if his memory returned, what then?

She eased her foot off the accelerator. Was she really going to be able to face talking about their lost baby?

She blinked back tears as her car came to a crunching halt outside the mansion which Giacomo had purchased lock, stock and barrel—with the carelessness of someone going out to buy a carton of milk. It was an exquisite dwelling—historically of great significance—and as different and as individually stunning as his Milanese apartment, his beach house in the Hamptons, or his magnificent house on the Amalfi coast. Throughout his adult life the billionaire tycoon had acquired and disposed of properties all around the world, at a breathtaking rate. He'd once told her, in a rare moment of confidence, that he was making up for having slept twenty-four to a room in his childhood orphanage.

His portfolio was undoubtedly impressive and envied by his peers, but he had a reputation for being a wealthy nomad. A man who moved between his costly residences without ever thinking of one in particular as home. They said that home was where the heart was, but Giacomo had no heart.

And that was what she needed to remember.

Tugging her suitcase from the boot, she made her way towards the entrance, but before she'd had a chance to knock the heavy door swung open and there was her estranged husband, standing silhouetted against the soft lighting of the panelled wooden hall, his powerful body dominating her line of vision and already doing crazy things to her pulse-rate. As he took a step back she could see him better, and the breath caught at the back of her throat. His black hair gleamed raven-blue in the soft light. His muscular forearm rested on the arching shape of the door frame. He looked like a study in virility and power as he stood there, his gaze unhurried as it surveyed her.

And Louise could do nothing about the sudden sweet clench of awareness low in her belly, or the instinctive tightening of her breasts—mercifully hidden by her anorak.

'You're late,' he accused softly.

If this were any normal working relationship she might have made some comment about the packed Christmas traffic and icy roads. But there was nothing remotely normal about this relationship. She didn't have to pretend or be super polite as she would to a brand-new, unknown client. It was really quite liberating. Maybe she needed to concentrate on that. 'Did you think I wasn't coming?'

He shrugged. 'I thought you might have changed your mind.'

'And would that have bothered you?'

Giacomo's eyes narrowed as he acknowledged the faint challenge in her voice. He could easily have brushed off her question, with its implied suggestion that he was somehow relying on her, but the truth was that her no-show *would* have bothered him. And what was the point of putting himself through this bizarre exercise, if he was going to conceal the truth with subterfuge? She was a puzzle to him. An enigma. If he unlocked her—as a thief might unlock a safe—then surely it would set his mind free and bring back the missing months? And wasn't that worth the minor inconvenience of being around a woman whom he found more than a little unsettling, for reasons he couldn't quite work out? 'I hate it if anyone reneges on a deal,' he offered coldly.

'Well, as you can see, I have stayed true to it. And it's very chilly out here. Aren't you going to ask me inside?'

'Of course.' Giacomo gritted her a smile as he opened the door wider. How strange that none of the usual conventions seemed to apply. He must have been more pleased to see her than he'd thought. He hadn't even noticed that he was standing there in his shirt sleeves and that his skin had begun to ice with goosebumps, although he observed that she looked warm enough in the same bulky and extremely unflattering jacket she'd worn the other night in the pub. Surely she had more than one coat? He frowned. Her shiny hair was tied back in a ponytail and, once again, she wasn't wearing a scrap of make-up. She certainly couldn't be accused of making a big effort for his sake!

He stepped back to let her enter, unprepared for the sudden onslaught to his senses as she passed by. She was close enough to touch and he surprised himself by how much he wanted to. Because her scent was tantalising. Faint and almost imperceptible—it contained the hint of oranges and sunshine. It was the most subtle and most provocative thing he had encountered in way too long and he could feel the hard clench of desire at his groin.

When had he last had sex with a woman? he wondered. Had it been with her?

Shutting the door on the cold air, he watched as she stood very still in the centre of the wood-panelled hallway and looked around. The antique wall lights were subtle but they provided enough illumination for him to see the sudden consternation which flitted indigo shadows across her pale face. 'You've been here before,' he said suddenly.

Louise nodded because suddenly she could barely speak, the lump in her throat making her feel as though she couldn't breathe. Had she really thought that she would be immune to the power of the past and the dangerous weave of her memories? 'Once,' she said.

'Was it for anything in particular?'

She kept her expression as neutral as possible.

'We came here not long after we were married. We spent our first Christmas here. Our only Christmas.'

'Ah.'

Breathlessly she waited for a flicker of recall or at least some acknowledgement that she had said something significant. But if she was hoping for some kind of profound reaction, then she was about to be disappointed.

'Does it look very different?' he questioned, as if he were an estate agent eliciting her opinion on some renovation work which had been done in her absence.

Louise attempted to answer with that same air of indifference. They'd spent barely any time here—a few days at most—but surely it was the same with any place. It wasn't the exterior and the trappings you remembered, but the things which had happened within those walls. It wasn't the structure or the costly contents, it was the *associations*.

And wasn't it inevitable that she should remember the moment she had married him, when the happy marriage she had hoped for had felt achievable? When she had vowed to love her handsome though often forbidding groom for the rest of her life and the prospect of that had shimmered before her, precious as gold. She, who had never really experienced love or a real home, had hoped that now she had both. Yet it hadn't happened, had it? Giacomo hadn't been able to commit to their relationship as she had thought a husband should, and had never let her get close enough for her to discover why. Her questions had been unwanted and unanswered. She had felt gauche for even asking them—as if she had stepped above and beyond the role which had been assigned to her.

'You don't remember our wedding?' she said.

'No.'

There was something so unequivocal about his reply that Louise grew very still, horrified comprehension dawning on her as she recalled the way he had looked at her when he'd been waiting in the office. The way he was looking at her now. With a look which was blank and stony. But suddenly she realised that his expression wasn't anger or judgement, as she'd initially thought. The reason was much simpler. And more than a little scary.

'You don't remember me either, do you?'

He dragged in a deep breath, then shook his head. 'No.'

A shudder ran through her body. 'Nothing at all?'

His black eyes were very intense. 'You want me to be honest?'

'Why else am I here, Giacomo? Is there any point in being anything but honest?'

'I guess not.' He expelled a long breath of air. 'You look like a stranger to me, Louise. When you walked into your office the other day, it was as if I'd never laid eyes on you before. You weren't…'

'Weren't…what?' she quizzed unsteadily as his words tailed off.

'Well, let's just say you weren't what I was expecting. You aren't the type of woman I usually go for.'

The sharp spear of pain which followed this entirely truthful remark warned Louise that she ought to be careful about asking questions if she couldn't bear to hear the answers. She wondered if that was mockery she could hear in his voice and if he intended her to feel *less than*. But he could only make her feel a certain way if she let him. So don't. 'How do you know that?' she questioned carefully.

'There are plenty of photos out there on the Internet. Paparazzi shots, mostly.' He paused, his shadowed gaze questioning. 'Though none of you. Not one. Not even on our wedding day.'

Louise hesitated. She had one on her phone, which she couldn't bear to delete. There were two, actually—although the second was a bit blurred. It should have been easy to pull it from her pocket and offer to show them to him but something stopped her, and that something was her own vulnerability.

He didn't remember her. Her face was a mystery to him. He'd even sounded as if he was comparing her unfavourably to all those amazing supermodels he used to date before she had fallen so easily into bed with him.

She guessed she would have to show him the

photo—but not yet. And not here. Not when she was standing with her scruffy little suitcase feeling a sense of hurt she had no right to feel. 'It was a very low-key affair,' she said and then looked at him with sudden appeal in her eyes. 'How the hell is this going to work, Giacomo? I mean, I know all these things that happened—am I supposed to just come out straight out and tell you about them?'

'No,' he said forcefully, his black eyes glittering. 'That's exactly what I don't want. Don't you think I could have pieced together all the events of the past for myself? That I don't have the wherewithal to employ someone to discover my movements and actions over the missing year and provide me with a detailed report? But I deliberately haven't done that. I've avoided an information dump which could overload my brain. I want to discover what happened for myself…organically. All I need is for you to answer my questions—as truthfully and as objectively as possible.'

So did that mean she was banned from saying that she thought he'd been a neglectful and inconsiderate bastard at times during their marriage? Would that sort of view be considered too subjective?

'Does that mean you'll answer mine in return?' she said. 'Isn't that only fair?'

His black eyes gleamed. 'Is that what you want?'

'I...think so. It could give me my own sense of closure.'

'And is closure what you seek?'

She swallowed. 'Of course it is.'

She glanced behind him, as if suddenly becoming aware of the loud tick of the grandfather clock and the faint crackle and splutter of a fire coming from a distant room. She shook her head like someone emerging from a long sleep as she attempted to confront this strange new reality. 'And in the meantime, you'd better tell me where I'll be sleeping.'

His body tensed. It was only the most fractional of movements but enough for Louise to notice. Perhaps he wasn't quite as indifferent to her as she had imagined, before dismissing the thought—because what good would it do her if she started thinking about sex?

'It seemed unnecessary to put you in one of the servants' rooms, under the circumstances.' His smile was bland. 'You can have the blue guest suite.'

Louise looked at him askance. There were plenty of other guest rooms he could have offered. Did he really expect her to sleep in the blue suite—while he lay next door, in the vast master bedroom they'd once shared? Did he really think she wouldn't *care*? She might have blamed his insensitivity on his accident until she reminded herself that this kind of behaviour was hardly new. He didn't even realise he was doing it. He was callous and unfeeling.

'Actually, it's probably best to stick to our delineated roles as much as possible,' she said smoothly. 'Less confusing that way. I'd prefer to sleep in one of the unoccupied servants' rooms.' She tilted her chin. 'So which one?'

'Don't be ridiculous, Louise. Taking that kind of proud, posturing stance is completely unnecessary,' he snapped.

'Let me be the judge of that. Which one?' she repeated calmly.

She saw the frustration which burned in his black eyes.

'I'll show you,' he bit out eventually.

'There's no need. Honestly. I can find it perfectly well by myself if you give me directions. Is it on the second floor, or the third?'

'No, Louise,' he said, with a steely determination she recognised of old. 'On this, I must insist.' He picked up her suitcase and walked out of the hall, obviously expecting her to follow and, with little other choice, she did.

Giacomo could feel the shimmer of anger and exasperation, and was aware of a sudden sense of disconnect as he led her up the sweeping staircase towards the very top of the house and one of the unused servants' rooms. It felt wrong to put her up here, but she was only taking him at his word, wasn't she? He had employed her as a housekeeper and she was behaving like one. But, oh, had she always been this stubborn?

He pushed open the door and looked around, acknowledging the rustic simplicity of the small room. A single washbasin stood in one corner and there was a compact desk in the other. A chair and a single bed were the only other furniture and the walls were plain and unadorned. He heard her suck in a breath, before walking over to the window to stare at the darkening landscape at the back of the house.

'Changed your mind now you've seen it?' he questioned mockingly.

She sounded as if she was speaking from between gritted teeth.

'Honestly, Giacomo—it really isn't important. I don't particularly care where I sleep. I'm only going to be here for a few days.'

But then she turned round to face him and all his frustrations trickled away, their battle of wills temporarily eclipsed by a very different type of frustration. Suddenly Giacomo was struck by how confined this space felt with two people in it, and how close she was. And once again something about her faint scent stirred his senses in a way which was unexpectedly potent.

His mouth dried. He had grown up in appallingly

cramped circumstances—the run-down orphanage had been dangerously overcrowded—yet never could he remember feeling quite as claustrophobic as he did right then. It felt as if the walls were closing in on them. It felt as if he had fallen into a trap, and yet instead of fighting his way out of it, which would be his natural instinct, he would be happy to let that happen. For their bodies to be sandwiched together in a sweet collision which would lead to only one thing—mostly involved with tumbling her down on that stupidly narrow bed and removing her clothes as quickly as possible. He stared at her parted lips, badly wanting to taste them and then to spread those slender thighs and lose himself deep inside her.

He pressed his thumb into his temple, trying to remember when he had last sought pleasure in a woman. When had he even *wanted* that? And how ironic that should be for the man whose libido had once been legendary—even if he had turned down most of the women who had regularly thrown themselves at him throughout his adult life. These days his body felt more like a machine. A cold and sexless machine. Dead from the waist down.

But he was lucky to be alive, wasn't he? That was the mantra he had repeated to himself over and over again, even if sometimes it felt like scant consolation for the memory and the desire he had lost.

But now?

Now he was experiencing something very different. Desire was rushing through his body like a flood of water over a desert plain, obliterating everything else in its path and, oh, it was deliciously sweet.

She had removed her bulky anorak and as she hung it on the back of the door he was able to observe her more closely. Her simple sweater and knee-length skirt were a suitable choice of clothes for someone who was being employed as a housekeeper, although he had imagined feminine pride might have made her choose something more flattering. Yet the simple garments complemented the curve of her hips and the lush swell of her breasts. He realised he must have touched and kissed those breasts many times, but he couldn't remember a thing about them—and that was more than a little distracting.

Her cheeks were lit with roses from the cold air outside and a couple of strands of dark hair had fallen down. And for some reason that natural disarray sparked his sexual hunger more than anything else. Had she been an abandoned lover? he wondered, though on some subliminal level he knew the answer to be yes. As she met his gaze her eyes darkened and her lips parted, as if she was silently acknowledging the almost tangible desire which was pulsing between them. He wondered how she would react if he pulled her against his rapidly hardening body and plundered those soft lips with his kiss.

He let out a ragged sigh. On one level he recognised that this development was a complication neither of them needed, yet wasn't it gratifying to know his body was still capable of responding like this? That after all the deadness and pain of the past should come lust, hovering like a vibrant interloper on the edges of awareness and making him remember what it was like to be truly *alive*?

He had told her that he would ask the questions because he had wanted to be the one in control. But wasn't this sudden surge of desire making him feel even more powerless? With an effort, he diverted his thoughts away from the clamour of his body, forcing himself to behave as if she really were his housekeeper. 'Dinner at eight?' he questioned coolly.

'Funny how you always manage to make a question sound like a command, Giacomo. I'd forgotten that about you.'

'But presumably you were turned on by a masterful man, or you wouldn't have agreed to marry me?' Unapologetically, he shrugged. 'And surely it's entirely appropriate, given your current status as my employee.'

He held her gaze again, but this time the darkening in her eyes looked like distress, not desire. And Giacomo found himself turning away as he felt a shaft of pain shooting through him. Not the kind of pain he'd willingly endured as the doctors had knitted together his shattered bones, but another kind. The kind he had avoided since a childhood he remembered all too well, no matter how much he tried to blot it out.

Emotional pain.

How much did she know about him? he wondered bitterly. How much had he told her when he had inexplicably asked her to be his bride? Had he revealed the darkness which had made him into the man he was?

Without speaking another word, he left the room, but as he stepped into the coolness of the corridor his skin felt flushed—as if he had suddenly acquired a fever. He began to run down the stairs, possessed by an urgent need to put distance between them, aware of the pounding sound of his footsteps as they echoed through the large house.

But far louder was the thunder of his heart.

CHAPTER FOUR

AFTER GIACOMO HAD GONE, Louise sat down heavily on the narrow bed. Her legs were so wobbly they could barely support her and she felt weird. Well, who wouldn't? Not just because suddenly she found herself occupying a small corner of the house she'd once been mistress of, but because for a moment back then she had thought that her estranged husband was going to kiss her.

And hadn't she wanted that? For a few insane seconds, hadn't she prayed like mad for Giacomo to act on the hunger which had blazed in his eyes like a dark, burning flame and for him to take her in his arms? To crush her against a body which was taut and tight with sexual tension, just as her own had been. She'd even fantasised about him pushing her down on this narrow bed and peeling off her clothes with the impatient dexterity she remembered so well. Wouldn't it help ease the terrible aching deep inside her, if he filled her with his hardness once more and thrust into her until she was shuddering out his name?

But that would be dangerous on so many levels—and not just emotionally. Sex…frightened her, or, rather, the possible repercussions of sex did. She closed her eyes. She didn't want to think about it, or what it could do to her. She could never bear to live through that kind of experience again.

Drawing in a shaky breath, she unzipped her boots, before putting them neatly into the bottom of the small wardrobe. No, on balance it was a good thing Giacomo had left the room so abruptly with that remote, hard expression on his face. It had prevented the possibility of anything happening. But that didn't stop her having to blink back the stupid tears which were suddenly so close to the surface, though maybe that wasn't so surprising in view of what she had learnt.

Because Giacomo hadn't remembered her, or the wedding—and obviously he didn't have a clue about her unplanned pregnancy. How could she possibly tell him about the miscarriage she had endured all alone, while he was on the other side of the world, not even caring enough to pick up the phone to speak to her? What words could she use to tell him, which wouldn't sound like blame, or bitterness? And how could she go through that terrible pain herself, all over again?

You don't *have* to tell him about that, she reminded herself fiercely. He had told her very clearly what he did and didn't want. *He* was the one who was driving this agenda and asking the questions, and therefore he was the one setting the boundaries. He told her that he wanted to discover his past organically—so she should take him at his word and protect herself in the process.

But the thought sat uncomfortably with her as she washed and changed into her Posh Catering uniform, twisted her hair into an updo, then went downstairs to explore the possibilities of what she could make for dinner.

At least some things didn't change. The kitchen was exactly as she remembered it—a perfect central-casting creation of old-meets-new, all constructed in the best possible taste, as befitted its billionaire owner. There was a vast dresser filled with exquisite Italian pottery, a weathered old table and two very old-fashioned sinks, reclaimed from a rural farmhouse. At one end was a large leather sofa on which were scattered soft cushions embroidered with strawberries and fronds of leaves, which added an element of comfort to this most functional of rooms. Every appliance was top of the range, designed to blend in as much as possible with a house which had been built when the idea of hot and cold running water would have sounded like sorcery.

And fortunately, Louise knew how everything worked. She had insisted on no staff being present when her Italian groom had carried her over the threshold, with flakes of snow melting in his hair—even though technically they hadn't been on their honeymoon. She had explained with a certain fervour that she wanted to cook for him, like a 'real' wife, and that had made him laugh indulgently. Even now she could recall the glow of pleasure and triumph which had rippled through her as he had agreed to her unexpected request. She'd thought back then that she could be an influence within their marriage. That she could make his glittering world seem more normal—an illusion quickly destroyed once they'd settled into married life. Because she had quickly learned that Giacomo was the one who made all the decisions.

But hadn't she contributed to that dynamic? So dazed and blown away by the fact that someone like him had actually *made her his wife*, she had allowed herself to be swamped by the sheer force of his powerful personality. Sometimes it had felt like standing on the end of a pier in the face of a wind blowing in from the sea, which had threatened to flatten her.

She hunted through the fridges and store cupboards to find them as well stocked as Giacomo had told her they would be, knowing she could have created a feast, if not fit for a king, then certainly one which would be well received in any top-class restaurant. But she wasn't going to do that. She wanted to give the man she had married something she'd observed rich men rarely got. Something simple, which might remind him of the past he so desperately wanted to claw back.

She would make him fresh pasta.

She found a clean apron, tipped flour onto a board and then added the eggs one by one, mixing first with a fork and then with her fingers. She hadn't done this in a long time. Deliberately? Probably. It had been something she'd insisted on learning once she'd known that she was going to marry an Italian. She'd wanted to be his perfect wife but now she wondered if there was any such thing.

The movement of her fingers was rhythmic. It felt soothing and vaguely comforting—as if she were one of a long line connected to the different generations of women who had made this dish in his homeland.

She concocted a simple tomato sauce, made an accompanying fennel salad, grated some parmesan into a small dish and, shortly before eight, went into the smaller of the mansion's two dining rooms and lit the candles.

She could hear the howl of the wind outside and wandered over to one of the mullioned windows which overlooked the extensive parkland. It was so stark and wintry out there—the leafless trees only just visible, like silent sentries which loomed on the horizon. The sky appeared more swollen than it had done earlier but there was still no sign of snow. Please don't let it snow, she prayed, knowing that a white Christmas would be just one layer of poignancy too many. She thought how cold it must be out there and what a long way she was from anything or anyone. Just her and the man she had married, alone in this vast mansion.

But at least in here it was warm. Someone—presumably Giacomo—had lit the fire so that the spluttering logs splashed golden and crimson light over the oil paintings which adorned the walls. She laid the table, enjoying the gleam of crystal and antique silver on the polished table—giving the room a sense of history and of continuity which contrasted so sharply with her own rather wobbly emotional state.

'Louise?'

She must have been too deep in her thoughts to hear him, because the soft use of her name startled Louise out of her introspection and the knife she was holding clattered out of her hand onto the table as she turned to see Giacomo entering the room. Her body tightened with instinctive pleasure and there didn't seem to be anything she could do about it.

He wore a linen shirt the colour of cappuccino,

which was open at the neck, revealing a tantalising glimpse of silken olive flesh. The faded jeans had been replaced by a pair of exquisitely cut dark trousers, which hugged his narrow hips and emphasised the powerful shafts of his muscular legs. Even from this distance she could detect his soap—not aftershave. He never wore aftershave. And her throat dried with hunger, for his hair was still damp from the shower and that made her think about things she most definitely shouldn't be thinking about. Like the two of them standing in a steaming cubicle with a stream of water gushing over her breasts. The slick of his fingers between her legs, while she gasped out his name against his wet shoulder.

'You've changed,' she said, realising too late that the remark was way too informal for a housekeeper to make.

'So have you,' he commented softly, his gaze taking in her black trousers and fitted pink Posh Catering shirt, with the elaborate *PC* logo embroidered above one breast. 'Though you seem to have taken the concept of dressing for dinner rather less literally.'

'I'm serving it, Giacomo—not eating it.'

'Of course you're eating it. You will be joining me.'

'That's where you're wrong.' She shook her head. 'I won't.'

'Why not?' he questioned as he sat down at one end of the table.

The candlelight danced shadows over his face, the flickering flames highlighting the jagged scar and drawing her attention to the fact that his once-perfect face was now flawed. Yet the crazy thing was that Louise thought she'd never seen him looking more sexy, or more vital. Was that because he had *survived*, or because his buccaneer presence was making her ache for the physical intimacy she'd been without for so long?

With an effort she dragged her mind back to his question, though it was proving very difficult to concentrate. 'Because you've employed me as your housekeeper, not your dinner guest,' she gritted out, feeling her nipples pushing against her uniform shirt and hoping he hadn't noticed. 'And believe it or not, I don't usually eat with my clients when I'm working for them.'

'But you are here for other reasons than simply working for me. I employed you for a specific purpose and there are questions I need to ask,' he reminded her coolly. 'How is that supposed to work? Am I supposed to grab moments to quiz you between courses, while you make do with a hurried sandwich in the kitchen?'

'I'm afraid there are only two courses,' she returned sweetly. 'So don't get your hopes up.'

'Then why don't you lay another place for yourself, before bringing in the first one?' he suggested.

'It's that old question-as-command again,' she observed. 'Do I have a choice, Giacomo?'

'You know something, Louise?' he countered. 'I don't believe you do.'

Giacomo watched as she frowned before turning away—her irritation replacing the hunger which had been darkening her eyes just moments before and presumably the reason why her nipples had started tightening so alluringly beneath her shirt. And hadn't her very obvious desire been reciprocated in him, a hundred times over? He had stared at her—this unknown woman with the blue eyes and dark hair—and his groin had grown exquisitely hard.

Had he ever ached as much as this before? he wondered distractedly. Because he was quickly realising that rediscovered lust had a potency all of its own. What else could explain the inexplicable hunger he felt towards Louise? He had started to fantasise about what he might like to do to her and she to him, and his fantasies had been unbearably erotic and vivid. He wondered what kind of panties she was wearing and what sound she made when she came, even though on one level he knew that all this information was buried deep in his mind.

Should he have felt guilty about entertaining such lustful thoughts? Probably. Yet as she left the room he felt curiously devoid of any such sentiment. Surely it was no sin to desire your own wife, even if you couldn't actually recall marrying her.

He watched firelight dancing golden patterns over the ancient walls, although for once he felt no desire to pull out his phone to check the state of the international money markets. Had his near-death experience taught him that it was unnecessary to discover how many thousands of dollars he had accrued overnight? It must have done, for suddenly no thought preoccupied him as much as contemplating the shapely body of his housekeeper.

She returned a few moments later, busying herself with unloading dishes from the tray she carried, her movements swift and efficient, as if she couldn't wait to get the meal eaten and the evening over and done with. That, too, was a little unflattering, but all it did was heat the growing fever in his blood.

'Would you like wine as well as water?' she questioned.

He shook his head. His doctor had advised him to avoid alcohol, fearing it might impact the possible return of his memory. But that hadn't been a big ask. Never much of a drinker anyway, Giacomo hadn't been able to face the thought of losing any more control than he already had. He gestured towards the tumbler in front of him. 'Just water,' he growled.

She laid a place for herself and filled their glasses

before sitting down and pushing the food towards him, and Giacomo stilled as a scent of something evocative transported him from this ancient English dining room to the Italian city where he had made his first fortune. It provided the one thing which his massive wealth had all but obliterated—simplicity—and it was the most perfect meal imaginable. He ate with enjoyment before looking up and noticing she wasn't eating herself, but was watching him closely. Her blue eyes were narrowed, making the naturally thick black fringe of her lashes appear even more dramatic, and once again he realised she wasn't wearing a scrap of make-up.

And something stirred at the edges of his mind. A drift of memory as elusive as a feather on the breeze. He tried to reach out and capture it but the more he concentrated, the more it evaded him and in the end he gave up. Instead, he put his fork down and looked at her.

'This is good,' he said. 'Where did you learn to make pasta like this?'

'You can tell it's home-made?'

He raised his eyebrows. 'I'm Italian, Louise. Of course I can tell.'

'I'm self-taught,' she explained. 'Everything I've learned has been from books and online tutorials.' She took a sip of water. 'You probably don't need to know all the detail—'

'Why don't you let me be the judge of that?' he questioned coolly. 'How did you get started?'

'Do you ask all your housekeepers that question?'

'Please don't test my patience,' he instructed silkily.

'It's probably not the most exciting CV in the world.' She shrugged her shoulders a little awkwardly. 'From the age of sixteen I worked in restaurants and hotels and then a couple of years later, I was offered a job cooking and waitressing for Posh Catering. And that's where I've been ever since— except when I was married to you, of course.' She met the question in his eyes. 'You didn't want me to work and you didn't want me cooking. You said you had staff to do that.'

He winced as he registered the subtle barb. 'That sounds unspeakably arrogant of me.'

'Well, yes.'

'And you say that's how we met?'

She nodded. 'I was hardly going to run across you at a film premiere, was I?' she said drily.

'Do you want to tell me about our first meeting?'

A look of something uncomfortable passed over her face. 'Is that really necessary?'

'I think so. You agreed to answer any questions I might ask you,' he said, his cool tone disguising the fact that he hated the inequality of knowing she held information about him. About them. Information he was not privy to. It gave her a certain power and that did not sit comfortably with a man to whom personal power was the most precious thing on earth. 'How else am I supposed to remember?'

There was silence for a moment or two. 'I was waitressing in a private dining room in central London.'

'When would this have been?'

'The end of August, year before last. I was serving caviar to you and several other high-powered businessmen and terrified you'd notice the little stain which I'd spilled on my uniform shirt and not quite managed to remove.' She gave a slightly nervous laugh. 'Funny how it's always the inconsequential details you can remember, isn't it?'

'What else?' he probed, ignoring her obvious attempt to change the subject. 'How did it begin?'

'You looked at me.'

'I looked at you,' he repeated slowly, raising his eyebrows enquiringly. 'And?'

'And I looked at you.'

To his astonishment, he found a smile nudging the edges of his lips. 'This all sounds very promising, Louise—but at some point you really do need to give me more detail than that.'

Louise dug her fingernails into the palms of her hands as she registered his sardonic tone. Would it sound credible to explain that something powerful and irresistible had sizzled between such an unlikely couple as them? It had been unbelievable, really—hence her reluctance to recount it. She had never experienced anything like it. Not before and certainly not since. Looking at him now it was difficult to believe that this gorgeous man had been so enthralled by her, or that he'd spent so many nights in her miniature apartment, which was only slightly bigger than one of the bathrooms in his Milanese apartment. Sometimes she'd thought he seemed more relaxed in that humble environment of hers than in whichever vast London hotel suite he happened to be staying in, and where he sometimes took her. Though when she'd found out about his childhood years in the orphanage, his attitude sort of made sense.

'We couldn't seem to stop looking at each other,' she continued. 'Even though I was obviously trying not to stare because I was supposed to be working. One of your companions even remarked on your wavering attention and you said that it was an insult to a beautiful woman not to look at her.' Nobody had ever called her beautiful before. Had that careless flattery made her over-susceptible to his charm? 'When I finished, you were sitting outside waiting for me in a chauffeur-driven car. You offered me a lift home—'

'Which presumably you accepted.' He sat back in the chair. 'Did we have sex that night?'

She blushed, then hated herself for blushing. Why

should she feel ashamed about what had felt almost preordained—and so inevitable that she honestly hadn't been able to contemplate the thought of turning him down? She wished he hadn't said it so baldly. He'd made it sound almost biological. But he was just speaking the truth, wasn't he? And it probably had been like that. For him, anyway. Men took what they could, didn't they? That was what her aunt had always taught her. 'Yes,' she said reluctantly. 'We did.'

'And was that usual?'

'What do you mean, was it *usual*?'

'I think you know what I mean, Louise.' His dark brows were raised in arrogant query. 'Did you make a habit of accepting lifts home from your clients?'

Louise slammed her glass down so hard that water slopped over the side, but she didn't care about possible damage to the antique table because his implication was deeply insulting. But at least it reminded her of how haughty and arrogant and proud he could be.

'Of course, I'd forgotten that in the mind of someone like you—who would have been happier living in the Stone Age—there's one rule for men and another for women! Were you in the habit of copping off with waitresses whenever you went to a restaurant? If you must know, I had never done anything remotely like that before. It was totally out of character for me to fall straight into bed with a man.' She nearly confided that he had been the *only* man she'd ever been intimate with, but why tell him stuff it wasn't his business to know? Why feed his insufferable ego? Hadn't she told him too much already?

'Then…why?' He looked taken aback. 'Why me?'

Was this fake modesty? she wondered bitterly. 'Why do you think, Giacomo? It can't have been a novel experience for a man like you. You're a very attractive man, as I'm sure you know. Plus, you're a great kisser and I got carried away. I couldn't resist you.'

'You're saying I took advantage of you?' he questioned furiously.

'*No!*' She shook her head. 'That's not how it was. We were equals. Or at least, that's how it felt at the time.'

Not afterwards, of course. Afterwards she'd realised just how unequal they really were and not just because she'd been an innocent and he a deliciously experienced lover. He was also one of the richest men in the world. She had quickly learnt that the waitress who had been plucked from obscurity and catapulted into the billionaire's super-privileged world would be expected to behave in a certain way. Namely, that she was simply supposed to slot into his life and not make any waves. That she was a fairly insignificant little cog in the very complex operation which maintained Giacomo Volterra's impossibly busy schedule. From being the object of his lust and adoration, she had gone to feeling practically invisible. Why else had he insisted on such a quiet wedding, and then such a low-key life when they'd moved to Milan?

'Then what? Are you trying to say we fell in *love*?' he said, sounding as if he were reading from a script.

The disbelief in his voice said it all. As if he doubted the existence of love. Which he did—he'd told her that, too—and maybe that was understandable. The few times when he'd reluctantly referred to his upbringing had made Louise's heart want to break for him. He'd certainly never told her he loved her—and, on the few occasions when she'd blurted it out to him, he had winced slightly, as if she had committed some dreadful faux pas.

She stared down at her barely touched food, tempted to tell him about the baby, but something stopped her and that something was her own deep sense of hurt. He hadn't wanted to talk about it at the time, had he? He had offered no comfort nor brought her any solace. She hadn't been able to reach him on the phone and by the time she had done it had been too late and she had already left the hospital. She'd been recuperating at his Milanese apartment—she'd never thought of it as hers—when he'd arrived back from New York in time for dinner and had surveyed her across the space of their dining-room table. A space which had suddenly felt as big as an airfield.

And she remembered exactly what he had said to her.

She pushed her plate away, her throat thick with dread and hurt and pain, but she forced herself to cling on to the positive—even though it was only the most fragile of threads. Because there had definitely been something else between them, especially at first. And Giacomo must have made her his wife for other reasons than an unplanned pregnancy, or because he'd never had a father of his own. Powerful billionaires must often find themselves in the position of becoming unexpected fathers, but these days they didn't necessarily have to commit themselves to marriage. She had told herself this many times before in the past—though, with the best will in the world, she didn't really believe it.

'There was definitely a spark between us. You said I made you laugh, which was rare,' she said. 'Though you told me a few days later that it was never intended to be anything more than one night—'

'*Did* I?' His stony black eyes narrowed. 'That was fairly brutal.'

'Oh, that was nothing!'

He'd also confided that the sex had been surprisingly good, despite her innocence. And had explained—quite kindly, she'd thought at the time, though in retrospect it had definitely been patronising—that he wasn't looking for commitment.

'You said you never gave a woman false hope and that you definitely weren't husband material.' She shrugged awkwardly. 'But you kept coming back.'

'For more?'

She flushed at his candour. 'I suppose so. You said I was a hunger you couldn't seem to satisfy. And then one day you said: *"Maybe marriage will be good for me."'* Her laugh sounded high. Forced. 'It sounded like an experience you had yet to tick off the list. You said you liked talking to me—so perhaps deep down you wanted me to play some sort of therapy role. But the trouble with that is that you're supposed to talk about deep stuff with your therapist, which you never did.'

'No,' he said, his voice flat, as if this didn't surprise him.

'Anyway...' She stood up, aware that if she wasn't careful he might notice the faint tremble of her fingers. 'I think that's enough for one night, don't you? There are things I need to do in the kitchen.'

'Louise, please sit down.'

Did he think she could just confide in him and lay out everything from their painful past and not be affected by it? That she would jump to attention whenever he snapped his fingers? 'No,' she said vehemently. 'I don't want to sit down. You can't turn me on and off like a tap, Giacomo. Yes, I've agreed to help you, but I think we might need to ration these sessions. You might not be fazed by talking about this stuff but I'm finding it, well…difficult.'

She didn't wait for an answer, just grabbed the congealing dish of pasta and hurried towards the welcoming warmth of the kitchen where she viciously scraped the leftovers into the bin. She blinked the sting of tears from her eyes as she stood at the sink, seeking comfort from plunging her hands into the hot, soapy water, but comfort seemed in short supply.

And then she sensed rather than felt him behind her and felt her body stiffen. She hadn't heard him enter the kitchen and she didn't want him there.

Yes, you do. You know you do.

'Louise.'

She didn't want him to sound gentle like that either, because that was a total misrepresentation. He'd rarely been gentle towards her before. She didn't need to be reminded of all the different ways he could make her feel. Helpless. Strong. Amazing. She closed her eyes and prayed that all traces of her tears had disappeared. 'Go away,' she whispered.

'Is that what you want?' he questioned.

She could have said yes. She definitely should have said yes, but his voice was like velvet whispering over gravel and suddenly all Louise could think about was how it felt to have him kiss her. To remember the way his lips had the power to wipe everything from her mind and leave in its place nothing but a blinding and incandescent pleasure. She wanted that now, but it would be wrong. She couldn't justify it with the newness and wonder she'd felt when she first met him, or the sense of being hit by a gigantic thunderbolt which robbed you of all choice and reason. She couldn't pretend that this would be anything other than a potentially dangerous sexual hunger, which would chew her up from the inside and then spit her out.

She huffed out a sigh. They had agreed to be truthful so how could she possibly tell him a lie—especially when desire must have been written all over her face? So get rid of it. Compose yourself. Think of what's important.

And having Giacomo kiss you doesn't even feature on that list.

'You shouldn't ask me what I want,' she said, in a low voice, turning round so her back was against the sink. 'It puts me at a disadvantage.'

'Not just you,' he said, inexplicably. He shook his head. 'I don't think I've ever felt quite so disadvantaged in my life. I'm trying to understand, Louise.'

'Understand *what*, exactly?' she breathed.

It was a challenge which Giacomo instinctively knew he would have quashed quite ruthlessly in the past. But somehow he recognised that he couldn't move forward until he had looked back. And even though Louise was at times unable to disguise the attraction she still felt for him, she sounded angry, too. Almost *bitter*. It was true that some of the things she'd told him tonight had made him sound like an unreasonable, even prejudiced man—but he had never had any complaints from the opposite sex before. Quite the contrary. He'd practically had to fight them off.

And then he had met Louise and married her. He frowned. What had been so special about her?

He reached out and put his hand on her arm, which was still damp, and he could feel her tense. It was probably the most innocent touch of his adult life, yet he could feel a powerful wave of something indefinable flowing between them. 'Everything,' he said simply. 'I want to understand everything.'

Louise couldn't move. She was frozen to the spot, as vulnerable as the first time he'd touched her, though now it was nothing more than his fingers pressing lightly against her skin.

But none of that old chemistry had gone. It combusted the moment his flesh made contact with hers, despite the outward innocence of what he was doing. It felt like reassurance. Like comfort. Like all the things he'd never offered to her before—and, unsurprisingly, they were very potent. It made her want to take it further. To slide into his arms and stay there. Desire was wrapping itself around her, luring her irresistibly towards him with its subtle, silken snare and she could feel something shift and change in the atmosphere between them.

She could imagine what might happen if she gave in to it. He would pull her into his arms and kiss her, and that kiss would quickly get out of hand, the way it always did. He would unbutton her uniform shirt and incite her throbbing nipple through the constricting lace of a bra which suddenly felt too small for her. He might even push her against the weathered old table with a hungry growl, and sweep away all the debris from the meal before letting it smash to the floor. And then what? Would he lay her down on its hard surface and have sex with her, without further preliminary—with her eagerly urging him on? It wouldn't be the first time it had happened.

At what precise moment did she realise that she was in danger of acting out her rampant thoughts? Was it as she shifted her weight to take an almost automatic step forward? And that was when her breath froze in her throat and her heart slammed hard against her ribcage. What was she *doing*? Had she lost her mind—or was she just programmed to react this way whenever this powerfully attractive man touched her? She had behaved impulsively the first time she'd met him and she was not going to repeat that behaviour. She was not going to be intimate with him.

Not now.

Not ever.

Not unless she wanted her emotions to become even *more* shredded.

Quickly, she moved to the other side of the kitchen and once she was safely away from the tantalising distraction of his proximity, she was able to conjure up a cool smile from somewhere. 'Well, good luck with that,' she said blandly, as if that wordless sensual interchange had never happened. 'Understanding *everything* is a big ask, but I'm sure that if anyone can do it, it's you, Giacomo.'

'Your faith in me is touching, Louise.'

Their gazes clashed.

'Would you...would you like coffee?' she questioned awkwardly, as reality readjusted itself and she regarded him through the eyes of a housekeeper, rather than those of a hurt and aching spouse.

'Please.' His eyes glittered. 'Perhaps you'd care to bring it to my office?'

CHAPTER FIVE

GIACOMO COULDN'T SLEEP.

Tossing and turning amid the rumpled sheets, he spent the long hours of the night unable to shake off the feeling of…

Turning onto his back, he stared up at the ceiling. What?

He wasn't sure. Last night he had wanted to ravish his wife where she stood in the kitchen but instead he had exercised a tight self-restraint. Yet despite the powerful sexual hunger which had pulsed between them, Louise had not acted on it either. She had primly moved herself away to the opposite side of the kitchen and regarded him with watchful eyes. Why was she so wary of him? Had he been cruel to her—unwittingly or otherwise?

But his preoccupation with memory soon gave way to the much more immediate demands of his body. An icy shower before turning in for the night had failed to quell the fierce ache which had been burning inside him, as did catching up on a couple of hours' work which could easily have waited until after Christmas. He realised that this was the first time in his life he had ever experienced sexual frustration. In the darkness, he gave a wry smile. Perhaps the experience might prove useful.

He thought back to when he'd lain in that expensive Swiss clinic and a stream of ex-lovers had got in touch, and for a short while he had read their emails and listened to their voice messages. Women he had known before his marriage and his accident, whom he remembered with a curiously impartial clarity. Amazing blondes, with gym-honed legs which promised paradise. One in particular he hadn't seen in years—now one of Hollywood's most famous movie stars—who'd sent him a saccharine card belying the brazen offer inside to sneak into the clinic and give him a blow job.

He had been outraged by the suggestion and the others had left him cold. Every single one of them.

He had banned all such further contact unless *he* was the instigator and that was when he had discovered his brief, below-the-radar marriage and had informed his aide that he intended to seek out his estranged wife. But Paolo had seemed almost *grudging* when he had presented Giacomo with the information needed to find Louise. And he had said the strangest thing.

Don't hurt her, boss.

Giacomo had been at first angry and then indignant. As if he would ever hurt a woman! In his opinion, women allowed themselves to be hurt, when they refused to accept the emotional limitations of a relationship, which he had always set out right from the beginning. But this woman he had married—she must have been much more than just a lover. He frowned. Did that mean that he had cared for her in a way which was special? This stubborn, dark-haired housekeeper who last night had set his blood on fire?

He remembered when he had touched her the night before and something dark and forgotten stirred inside him. But once again it eluded him.

In the end he gave up trying to sleep and waited until the wintry dawn was painting the sky with pale shades of monochrome. He gazed out of the window to see that the expected snow had not materialised and for that he was grateful, for he still had flashbacks about pristine white wastes covered in the crimson flowering of his own blood, which had followed his skiing accident.

He took a long shower and dressed—making himself a jug of strong coffee and taking a deep slug of it before sliding his laptop into his briefcase. The grandfather clock in the hall was chiming eight and he was just pulling on his heavy cashmere coat when he heard Louise moving around upstairs, and he automatically tensed as he heard her soft footfall on the stairs.

'Oh,' she said as she came into view halfway down the staircase, standing stock-still as if he had just put a spell on her and turned her to stone. She cast her gaze over his coat and his briefcase. 'Are you going out?'

Giacomo tried to be objective but how could he possibly do that when her stillness made it all too easy to drink her in? Her dark hair looked rich and glossy and he itched to remove the constricting pins and let it fall in a silken tumble around his fingers. Her body looked firm and delicious and, even though she was wearing that unprepossessing uniform, all he could think about was undoing the buttons of her pink shirt and touching the delicious breasts which lay beneath.

'Were you a detective in a former life?' he questioned sardonically.

Reaching the bottom of the staircase, she pleated her brow together, as if she had decided to ignore his sarcasm. 'It's just…well, you said you wanted to talk and stuff and I'm only here until Boxing Day. That doesn't give us a lot of time.'

'Maybe you should have thought about that when you turned up so late yesterday. But it can't be helped. I'm taking the train up to London and it's something I can't get out of,' he informed her abruptly.

'On Christmas Eve?' She frowned and then the rather sniped words fired out, as if she couldn't prevent herself from saying them. 'Important lunch date?'

He gave a thin smile in response. 'It was the one day when I could get an appointment with my doctor.'

She looked momentarily taken-aback. 'I'm not surprised. Most people will be out doing last-minute bits of shopping or putting the tree up.'

'Then I must give thanks that I am not most people,' he observed drily.

Her blue eyes were suddenly watchful. 'You look tired,' she observed, before chewing on her bottom lip. 'I'm sorry. That's none of my business.'

'I can't think what on earth kept me awake,' he answered softly. 'When ordinarily I sleep like a baby.'

The colour had completely drained from her face and her eyes had clouded with what looked like acute distress. Was she really so super-sensitive about him making an oblique reference to the undeniable sexual chemistry which had fizzed between them?

'Shall I make you some breakfast before you go?' she questioned.

The voice was even more prim now and Giacomo

glanced at his watch. Maybe it was a good thing he was going to be out all day, if she was going to be as prickly as this.

'I'll pass. My taxi will be here any minute. I'll be back around five,' he added as he opened the door, his attention caught by the sight of pale flakes floating past. *'Dannazione,'* he swore softly. 'It's snowing.'

After he'd gone, Louise went into the kitchen, her head all over the place—unable to forget last night's blissfully disturbing moment in the kitchen. And then Giacomo had added to her discomfiture by making that throwaway remark about sleeping like a baby. She shuddered out a sigh. Of course he wouldn't have a clue that his unwitting words had stabbed like a knife to her chest and not just because he didn't remember their own baby. Because fatherhood had never been high on his list of priorities, had it? He'd barely mentioned the tiny life growing inside her, even when she had been pregnant. He had never wanted to discuss names, or even decide where they were going to position the crib in his Milanese apartment.

But she wasn't here to think about the way he'd behaved in the past. She was here to help him remember. So, rather than drifting around the place feeling useless pangs of sorrow and regret, how was she going to achieve that?

She poured some lukewarm coffee from the jug he must have made earlier and absently put a slice of bread in the toaster, because something he'd said in the Posh Catering office the other day had given her an idea.

I'm no fan of Christmas.

She knew that anyway and she knew why. Soon after they were married he'd explained that life at the orphanage had been especially grim during Christmas. It was the one time of year when gifts had flooded in for those deprived and lonely boys, but Giacomo hadn't wanted people's pity—or their charity.

His voice had been flat and definitive as he had given her this rare insight into his character and his past, but Louise had been on such a high with emotion that she had pleaded with him to have their own tree—because their first Christmas as a married couple *needed* a tree. And Giacomo must have been feeling indulgent at the time, because he had kissed her very softly and agreed.

It had been the only time during their short marriage when she had actually acted like a billionaire's wife—waltzing into one of Knightsbridge's fanciest department stores and letting her imagination run riot. She had been like a child in a sweet shop as she purchased festive baubles and ornaments and arranged to have them delivered to his country mansion. And while she had been busy shopping, so had Giacomo. He had bought her a necklace to place beneath that fragrant fir tree. A fine chain with a delicate star pendant—sparkling and studded with yellow diamonds which glittered like the Star of Bethlehem. She'd left it behind when she'd walked out of the marriage, along with all the other jewellery he'd bought her.

She wondered if he had kept the tree decorations. Would he have done that, or simply bundled up all evidence of her presence here and donated it to the local thrift store? The latter option, most probably. But what harm would it do to take a look? If she didn't find anything, she could always drive down to the village and see if there was anything left on the shelves. Because Christmas was a big deal, for all kinds of reasons. It stuck like glue to the mind, even if you hated it. If she used the right props to recreate their Christmas past, mightn't that prompt Giacomo's memory?

She finished her toast and went upstairs, reminding herself that first she needed to think about the present, which meant making her employer's bed, as any good housekeeper would. But that was easier said than done, to walk into the master bedroom which once she had shared with Giacomo and to stand beside his super-king bed. A lump rose in her throat. In this bed he had taught her to explore her sexuality and the wide gap in their levels of experience hadn't seemed to matter a bit. He had given her orgasm after incredible orgasm, transforming the blank canvas of her innocence into a vibrantly sensual landscape. And with every day that had passed, she had loved him a little more.

Being here again could have triggered a whole raft of emotions—humiliation and embarrassment being the obvious ones—but as Louise tugged the fine linen under-sheet of the enormous bed until it was as smooth as glass, she was aware of nothing other than an aching sense of regret. Why was that? Because he had pushed her love away with a slickness born of practice? Maybe. But it was too late to do anything about it now. Everyone knew that regrets were pointless.

She polished and cleaned the bathroom until it gleamed, then began exploring the bedrooms in search of the Christmas decorations, not really believing she might find them.

But in that she was wrong.

She found herself standing stock-still in one of the guest rooms, staring in disbelief at several cardboard boxes lying in the back of the large wardrobe. The branding of the Knightsbridge store was instantly recognisable, but it wasn't that which made Louise stop in her tracks. It was what she saw at the far end of the wardrobe and she narrowed her eyes in disbelief. A whole stack of clothes—*her* clothes—hanging in a neat line.

Her fingers were trembling as she touched the velvet and silk gowns, the cashmere sweaters and tailored pants. Beautiful clothes in luxurious fabrics. The sort of clothes you might wear to the theatre, or a party, but only if you were very, very rich. She'd left them here because she'd been planning to come back—during that brief window of time when anything had seemed possible. But she had never come back. Until now.

There were shoes, too—neatly stored in cardboard boxes—their toes stuffed with wads of tissue paper to keep them looking perfect. And drawers of gossamer-fine lingerie which had always made her feel decadent when she'd been wearing it—and even more decadent when Giacomo had slowly been removing it with that slow smile on his lips. That sense of disbelief lingered as she ran her hand over the shimmer of silk and delicate froth of lace.

Why had he kept them? Why had he clung to these remnants of a past he claimed not to remember?

She had walked out of their brief marriage with very little. Her Milanese designer clothes had felt hopelessly out of place after her return to England, so she'd sold them and lived off the proceeds until a vacancy had come up at Posh Catering. She had quickly recognised that the trinkets and accessories of a billionaire's wife would be hopelessly unsuitable for her normal life.

This life. Her life as it was now. The life she would return to once her job here was over, when she would be serving and clearing up after her wealthy clients rather than wasting time by being tugged towards a past which was gone for ever.

But at least the decorations she'd bought were intact—the only one she couldn't bear to open was the carved nativity scene with the miniature crib, because she honestly thought she might dissolve if she even glanced at the tiny baby, lying in a manger.

She straightened up and started thinking that maybe she could capitalise on all this. Was it too much to hope that if she drove down to the village there might still be a tree for sale? Wasn't Christmas supposed to be about hope?

Grabbing her anorak, she found her purse and car keys, and ten minutes later her little car was bumping its way over the cobbled stones of Westover high street, before grinding to a noisy halt outside the little greengrocery store.

It was still early. Too early for the last-minute Christmas shoppers who would soon descend on this upmarket little village in the Chilterns, with its tasteful festive traditions which went back years. She remembered that other Christmas Eve when Giacomo had brought her here late in the afternoon and they'd joined the small throng gathered around the giant tree in the square, as the daylight had faded and mothers had been trying to calm their over-excited children.

She had been a mother once.

Her eyes filled as she got out of the car.

Because didn't some cruel people think that mothers without children weren't really mothers at all?

Brushing an impatient fist over her eyes, she went towards the old-fashioned shop, which presented a Christmassy scene glowing enough to have made Charles Dickens drool. Outside, there were all manner of seasonal goodies. Bright orange pyramids of clementines. Boxes of walnuts and shiny dates. Bunches of mistletoe as big as bouquets, and spiky green holly studded with crimson berries.

And a single tree propped against the wall. It was a massive thing with rather sad and drooping branches at the bottom and the matronly assistant cast a doubtful eye over Louise when she asked how much it was.

'It's the last one,' she said, presumably to justify the astronomical price she quoted.

'I'll take it.'

'I've had trouble shifting it because it won't fit in the average house. You do realise it's nearly fourteen feet tall?' the woman added, before casting a doubtful eye over Louise's small car. 'And you'll never be able to get it in there.'

It was a masterclass in how *not* to sell something and Louise found herself smiling. 'It's for Barton.'

'Barton?' The eye-popping response was predictable. 'Ooh! Well, you won't have any trouble fitting it in *there*. Lucky girl to be working in that lovely house—and for that gorgeous man.' She smiled. 'Don't worry, dear, I can have it delivered soon after lunch.'

Louise reached in her bag and paid for the tree, some scarlet candles and a big bag of clementines, thinking she would get Giacomo to reimburse her for it later, as she would if he were any other client. She also told herself it was stupid to bristle at having been mistaken for a member of his staff. *Because what else was she, if not that?* Maybe she needed to get it into her thick skull that she fitted the role of Volterra housekeeper far better than she ever had the role of Volterra wife. She felt more at ease cleaning his sink than she'd ever done flying in his private jet.

She put the candles and clementines on the passenger seat and started up the engine, but now that some of her initial euphoria had worn off, a feeling of dread had started gathering like a small pile of pebbles at the pit of her stomach. The next couple of days had the potential to be painful, she recognised—for both of them. Especially if Giacomo got around to remembering that he'd only ever married her because she'd been carrying his child. She had wanted his baby so much, and had been left with nothing but an empty womb and a terrible aching deep inside her as she had done the only thing she *could* do—walked away from a man who had never really wanted to marry.

No, the next couple of days weren't going to be easy.

But surely far better to accept that and face it full on, no matter how much it hurt.

Because wasn't pain necessary for a wound to heal properly?

CHAPTER SIX

THE LAST OF the daylight had leeched from the sky and the clouds looked swollen as Giacomo made his way up the drive towards the house, through the pale swirl of snow which had just started to come down and was getting heavier by the second. In the distance he could see lights in the windows and spirals of smoke swirling from several of the ancient chimneys and his footsteps slowed as something unknown stabbed at his heart. Was his imagination playing tricks with him? Because from here it looked like a real house, not just a fancy shell or some plush illustration from an interiors magazine—which was how most of his homes had been described.

But none of them had ever felt like home.

His body tensed.

Except maybe once. He felt the flicker of something vaguely comforting. Had it been here, with Louise? He scowled as that elusive tug of memory taunted him yet again. Or was he just recalling some drug-induced hallucination after the accident when they'd pumped him full of morphine? He had despised that feeling. Had insisted on radically reducing his analgesia, to the astonishment of his medical team. But he had preferred the bite of pain to the sense of being out of control, because control was his old friend. It had driven him and protected him all his life.

And he wanted that feeling back again.

He reached the house and unlocked the front door and as he stepped into the panelled hallway and began to unbutton his overcoat, his senses were overloaded by the unfamiliar. It was warm in here— deliciously warm—and on some level he could detect the subtle fragrance of currants and spice scenting the air. Through the open door of the sitting room he could see the flickering glow and hear the crackle of the fire.

Suddenly Louise appeared at the doorway, looking a little flustered. She was still wearing that infernal uniform but behind the low bib of her flour-covered apron, she had undone a couple of shirt buttons—inexorably drawing his attention to the fecund swell of her breasts.

'I didn't hear the taxi,' she said.

'That's because I walked from the station.'

She was staring at his head, where he could feel the melt of snow, cold against his hair.

'It's bitter out there,' she said. 'You could have asked me to come and collect you.'

'I'm not sure I'd be able to fit my legs into that ridiculously small car of yours,' he drawled.

She smiled at this. *Madonna mia*, but it was a beautiful smile. How could he have forgotten *that*?

'And how did you get on? At the doctor's.'

From anyone else this would have been an impertinent query, but Giacomo was coming to realise that some of his old prejudices might impede his progress if he wasn't careful. He couldn't keep everything locked away if he wanted to liberate his mind—and surely if there was one person he could confide in, it was the woman he'd married.

'There was no silver bullet,' he admitted gruffly. 'The doctor put me through a series of fairly gruelling tests.'

'Don't tell me—you passed them all with flying colours?'

He acknowledged the mockery in her tone with the brief inclination of his head. 'The physical ones, yes. Of course.' But he remembered the latter part of the consultation, when he had demanded to know when he was going to get the missing year back.

'Still no progress there?' the medic had questioned, glancing up from his notes.

Giacomo had been about to say no when suddenly, in that Harley Street clinic, he had recalled the shimmer of Louise's eyes last night, and another image had pushed its way into the forefront of his mind. Of his wife getting up from the table of their Milanese apartment, with tears streaming down her face. It had been an unexpectedly real and disturbing recall. It had shaken him then and it was doing the same thing now.

And suddenly, it was as though a veil had been lifted from his vision and Giacomo narrowed his eyes. It was like one of those sped-up films of an artist drawing a face. Spare pencil strokes building into shadowed features. A curved line becoming a soft mouth he recognised all too well because he had kissed it before—many times. A tumble of dark, glossy hair which had once trickled like silk between his fingers.

'What is it?' she whispered. 'Why are you looking at me that way?'

For a moment he hesitated, instinctively knowing that in the past he might have kept this nugget of information to himself, because knowledge was power and power was what drove him. But he found himself wanting to tell her because it felt like a small, sweet victory.

'I've remembered,' he said slowly.

'How…how much?'

'Your face.'

There was a pause. 'And that's it?'

'Unfortunately, *sì*.'

He didn't think it would be appropriate if he added that he hoped some vivid recall of her body would soon follow.

Was that disappointment which crumpled her features? He didn't know but he was damned if he was going to discuss it now when he was standing in the hallway, all damp and covered in melting snow. His sudden recollection had left him feeling strangely *exposed* and that was something which didn't sit easily with him.

'I'm going upstairs to take a shower,' he growled.

'Of course.' She smoothed down her apron, as if silently acknowledging the resumption of their roles as employer and employee. 'Dinner at eight,' she responded formally.

Louise quickly turned away, not wanting to watch as Giacomo mounted the sweeping staircase. Things were changing and that was unsettling. She couldn't deny that she had watched the slow dawning of recognition which had briefly transformed his cold features. She had known that some fragment of recall had occurred, even before he'd told her that he remembered her face, and she'd felt a stupid glimmer of hope. But what had she been expecting? That in a sudden light-bulb moment he would declare she had been the woman of his dreams? She sighed. She had only ever been a body to him. Someone he liked to have sex with, who he had inadvertently made pregnant along the way.

But he had hurt her. He had hurt her badly.

And she would never let a man get close enough to hurt her like that again.

She went into the kitchen to check on the food and then into the dining room, where everything was prepared and waiting, unable to shake off a clawing feeling of anxiety. She looked around the beautiful room—deeply satisfied with the results of her handiwork, even while doubts were beginning to creep over her. Would Giacomo be angry at what she had done? How would the self-confessed 'no fan of Christmas' respond to being confronted by something which looked as if it had fallen straight from the pages of a seasonal fairy tale?

Standing in the window, reflected against a backdrop of falling snow, the giant tree looked magnificent—the giant silver star which glimmered at its tip almost touching the high ceiling. From the branches hung a profusion of delicate baubles which shone and danced and glittered. There were shimmering globes studded with tiny red stars and filigree silver bells which actually rang. Tartan ribbons adorned the scented boughs, and lights like miniature candles were looped around the fragrant branches. There was even a miniature fluffy snowman with a carrot for a nose and a little Santa Claus with a bulging sack full of presents. She'd bought those two because she'd imagined a future when the chubby little hand of their son or daughter might help decorate the tree. How far away that dreamed-of future seemed now.

Louise's throat tightened. The only thing she hadn't included had been the exquisitely made nativity scene which she'd left unopened in its box, but now she wondered if she was being an emotional coward by refusing to include it. Did she really have the right to censor the past, just because she was terrified of the effect it might have on *her*? Mightn't the sight of the little baby in a crib stir Giacomo's sleeping memory?

She went upstairs and quietly made her way towards the guest bedroom, intending to retrieve it. But just as she was reaching the end of the corridor, with its ancient and slightly creaking floorboards, she heard the sound of a door opening followed by that richly accented voice.

'Louise?'

It still sounded strange to have him call her that and yet it didn't stop her skin from shivering with a sense of loss and longing. Louise turned around, her reluctance to face him intensifying when she saw what he was wearing.

Her breath dried in her throat.

Very little.

In fact, he was nearly naked—with just a small white towel slung low over his narrow hips to shield his manhood. He was clearly not long out of the shower, his olive skin gleaming like oiled silk, and the microscopic droplets of water which glittered in his hair made it look as if someone had sprinkled a handful of diamonds over his dark head.

And Louise was instantly transfixed by his semi-naked appearance. She couldn't help herself. It was one thing knowing what you *should* do in circumstances like these—which was to hurry away—but quite another to put it into action when you were confronted by the reality.

Because the reality was that she was blown away by the sight of his magnificent body, with its underlying pulse of power. Her gaze roved over the long, muscular limbs. The toned torso. The honed abdomen and distracting line of dark hair which disappeared enticingly beneath the edge of the snowy towel. She seemed to have lost the ability to breathe or move. Her thoughts were scrambled as past and present fused into an erotic and confusing mixture and she felt her breasts prickle into delicious life as he subjected her to that lazy gaze which always used to turn her on so much.

'So what's this all about, Louise?' he taunted

softly. 'I thought your preference was to avoid the guest rooms.'

'I was looking for something.'

'What?' He slanted her a mocking look. 'Me?'

In a way she was grateful for his arrogance. It shocked her out of her erotic reverie and brought her crashing back down to earth. So stop fantasising and get real, she told herself fiercely, suddenly reminded of a useful distraction and a question she needed to ask him. She looked at him steadily. 'Why did you keep my clothes?'

'What are you talking about?' He frowned. 'What clothes?'

'The stuff I used to wear when we were…married. They're still here. In one of the rooms along the corridor.'

His scarred face was emotionless—with only the faint working of a nerve at his temple giving any indication that her disclosure might have ruffled him. 'How should I know? I haven't been here in two years,' he said coolly. 'I really don't think the staff would take it upon themselves to start removing your stuff just because we're no longer a couple, do you? Feel free to take any of it.'

Now why did that hurt so much? Why did his thoughtless comment make her want to rush up and strike him, or push him, or…or…?

'*Sì*, I know,' he said, very softly, a ragged kind of sigh leaving his lips as he nodded his damp head.

She blinked. 'What do you know?'

He shrugged. 'That the chemistry between us is off the scale.' He gave a short laugh. 'And maybe if we gave into it, it might help me to remember.'

Once again, his thoughtlessness meant she was able to match his careless tone. 'In your dreams, Giacomo.'

His smile was dangerous. Wolfish. How could she have forgotten the deliciously predatory nature of that smile?

'Funny you should say that,' he murmured. 'You had a starring role in them last night.'

And then, very deliberately, he turned his back on her and walked back towards the master bedroom and Louise very nearly gasped. Because now she could see that his back was scarred, too—only much more than his face. Ridged red lines criss-crossed over the oiled olive flesh, indicating just how badly he had been injured. Had he deliberately wanted her to see them?

And, oh, she had to stop herself from running towards him—but now she no longer wanted to strike him, or push him. She wanted to kiss every centimetre of that damaged skin and trace it with her fingertips and her tongue, reacquainting herself with this new version of her husband.

Who was not really her husband at all.

* * *

'What's going on?'

Giacomo's voice was quiet and tight, and he saw Louise's anxious look in response to his terse question.

'Isn't it obvious?' she questioned lightly. 'It's Christmas!'

A pulse pounded at his temple as he looked around the candlelit dining room, which was barely recognisable as the same place where he'd eaten dinner last night. Fairy lights twinkled and shimmered and hung from every available surface, so that the squashy velvet sofa looked as if a galaxy of stars had tumbled from the sky and surrounded it. Sprigs of holly festooned the top of every oil painting and some was massed in a giant centrepiece on the table, where yet more tall red candles flickered. Against the mullioned windows stood an absolute monster of a tree, hung with a profusion of decorations which even he would be forced to concede were unlikely to have originated from the local village shop. He felt the stir of something complicated and perplexing, but it felt too close to emotion for comfort and so he allowed the naturally logical side of his brain to swamp it.

'Where did all this come from?' he demanded.

'We...' She shrugged her shoulders. 'Well, *I* bought all these decorations in London for our first

Christmas here, not long after we were married. I was keen to do a traditional celebration and you were happy enough to let me. Actually, you gave me free rein. Told me to order whatever it was I wanted, so I did. I went looking for them on the off chance they might still be here, and they were. They've only been used once before and it seemed a pity to let them go to waste.' She hesitated. 'Do you...do you mind?'

His gaze switched from the decorations to her face and the way she was chewing her lip with obvious anxiety. He wanted to tell her that the room felt claustrophobic with all these unnecessary lights and baubles and glitter. That it was disconcerting to be reminded of a different Giacomo—a man who had tolerated Christmas and had obviously been feeling indulgent, possibly even tender towards his young bride. It was a difficult image to reconcile with the cold person he knew himself to be today but he bit back his automatic response, which was to tell her to get rid of them. It wasn't going to help his case if he snapped at her, or told her that this sort of over-the-top festive display had not been on his agenda. She was obviously seeking his approval, so perhaps he should give it—and barter for a little something in return.

'Let's just say I might be prepared to live with it if you were to enter into the spirit of the occasion yourself,' he said slowly.

She frowned. 'I'm not quite with you.'

'You talked about the clothes you found earlier?'

'Yes.'

'Then why don't you go and put on one of the dresses? It will certainly flatter you more than that—' he lifted the palms of his hands '—that *orribile* uniform. Wear one, Louise. For me. For old times' sake.' He paused. 'Can you think of a good reason why not?'

Her eyes narrowed in response to this, those thick black lashes fringing the extraordinary blue, and for a moment he observed the wariness which flickered in their depths and wondered what had put it there. What had happened between them?

'I guess not,' she said slowly.

He waited while she went upstairs to change, walking across the room to stare out of the window. The snow was coming down fast now and inevitably it made him think of the off-piste slope where he'd had his accident. It should have been an effortless ski run for a man of his sporting capability. But something had been playing on his mind that day. Something which had caused a split-second lapse of vital concentration. The tree had loomed up ahead seemingly without warning and then there had been nothing but the sickening smash of his body and stars exploding in his brain before everything went black.

He was relieved to have his thoughts diverted by Louise's reappearance, though wholly unprepared for her Cinderella-like transformation. The breath dried in his throat and he felt the urgent stab of desire at his groin. Her delicious curves were poured into a fitted dress of scarlet velvet, worn with a thin black belt which defined her narrow waist, making her look like an old-fashioned pin-up. A very sexy Mrs Santa. He felt a sudden urgent stab of lust. She was much taller in high black heels which showcased her shapely legs, and she had left her hair loose, so that it spilled like dark molasses over her narrow shoulders.

'Is this what you had in mind?' she questioned, in a strange voice.

Something flared in his mind. Something was missing.

'Wait here,' he said abruptly, ignoring her startled look—as if this wasn't the reaction she had been expecting.

He hurried to the safe which was kept in his office and opened it, half wondering if his scrambled thoughts were playing tricks on him. But when he returned to the dining room, he found her standing exactly where he'd left her, her face pale and tense—as if she were regretting having fallen in with his wishes. He handed her the box and she took it blankly.

'What's this?'

'Open it.'

Louise's ears were roaring as she flipped open the box to see a necklace lying on a bed of indigo velvet.

The most beautiful necklace she had ever seen and one she recognised instantly. A fine chain holding a delicate star pendant, studded with yellow diamonds, which sparkled like the Star of Bethlehem. It shouldn't have been a shock and yet it *was* a shock. It made some nameless feeling coil like a snake at the base of her stomach as she looked at him, not speaking—not daring to speak—her expression seeking explanation.

'You wore it with that dress once before,' he said slowly, taking the box away from her and putting it down on a nearby table. 'I bought it for you. For Christmas.'

'Yes. Yes, you did.' Suddenly she felt shaky, as if recognising that the return of his memory was probably going to be as poignant for her as it was for him. 'You said it would be a crime not to wear it with this dress and so you gave me the present early. Two... two years ago tonight.'

He nodded, a strange new note in his voice. 'Put it on.'

'Giacomo—'

'Put it on. Please. I want to see it. You will be joining me for dinner tonight, won't you, Louise?' His sensual lips curved into the mocking smile which had always blindsided her. 'And surely diamonds are preferable to the entwined initials of your damned catering company staring at me from the other side of the table.'

It was an order Louise knew she shouldn't refuse, no matter how much she questioned the wisdom of wearing his jewels again, but her hands were trembling too much to be able to deal efficiently with the catch and in the end Giacomo took over. It wasn't a lengthy operation but it felt like a blissful for ever as his fingers lifted the heavy pile of hair and he brushed his fingertips over the shiver of her skin. Tension fizzed in the air as the silence between them grew more intense. Every pore of her ached for him as he put his hands on her shoulders and turned her round, so that her image was reflected back at her in the mirror, as was his.

From here she could hardly recognise herself. The red dress. The diamond necklace. The loose cascade of hair. And Giacomo standing behind her, tall and dark and indomitable, his hands still on her shoulders—a gesture which seemed like a parody of possessiveness. She didn't look like the woman she had been before and yet she didn't look like the woman she was now, either. So where did that leave her? Confused, yes—but aching, too. Filled with a need for him which went deeper than just sexual desire. He was close enough to touch and she wanted him to kiss her. On some level she *needed* him to kiss her, even though she knew she'd be fast-tracking her way to yet more hurt if he did.

But he didn't.

He didn't even try.

She wondered if that was deliberate and if he was simply playing games and demonstrating his power over her. Was he clever enough to realise that it was human nature to want what you were being denied? That you could start the fiercest fire from the small-est smoulder? She licked her suddenly dry lips. And, oh, she was smouldering now. Her breasts were push-ing so hard against the soft red velvet that they felt as if they might explode.

So take back control, she told herself fiercely as she turned away from her candlelit reflection and the touch of his hands. She might have dressed up obedi-ently because he'd demanded it, but that didn't mean she had to start behaving like his tame puppy. And even though she was wearing velvet and diamonds— she was still nothing but his temporary housekeeper.

'If you'll excuse me, I have lots of things I need to do in the kitchen,' she said in a low voice.

'Of course,' he answered. 'I'll be working in my office until dinner. Text me when it's ready.'

His tone was as equable as hers—as if he were oblivious to the dark undercurrents which were flow-ing between them. But Louise could feel his gaze burning into her as she moved away from him and she only just resisted the urge to run from the room. Because she had run from him once before, and that was the reaction of a coward.

CHAPTER SEVEN

'LEAVE THAT.'

Louise's hand stilled as she was reaching for a porcelain bowl which contained the remains of some griddled aubergine. They had just eaten the most surreal Christmas Eve dinner imaginable—fortunately punctuated by several different courses, which meant she'd been able to keep jumping up from the table to bring in yet another dish. To her relief, this had kept conversation to a minimum and she had been about to clear the table when Giacomo's terse command suggested he had other ideas.

'I was about to fetch dessert.'

'I said leave it,' he growled. 'I don't want dessert. Do you?'

Keep it light and professional, she told herself. It was safer that way. Because she felt conflicted, slipping back into housekeeper mode when she was dressed like a rich man's wife.

She was finding it difficult to control her thoughts—and her feelings. She needed to protect herself—mostly from her own stupid desires— because she was way more vulnerable around Giacomo Volterra than she'd thought.

'Not particularly,' she said, shrugging her shoulders in an attempt to adopt a convincing air of nonchalance. 'But it's slightly annoying to think I've spent all afternoon making *struffoli* and you're not even going to try it.'

'You've made *struffoli*?'

'Of course I haven't! I know it's what Italians traditionally eat on Christmas Eve but that would have taken me all day, and then some—and as you can see, I've been busy with other things.' She hesitated. 'I've… I've actually prepared you an orange.'

He stilled. 'Why an orange?'

Her mouth dried as she remembered what he'd once told her. 'You said it was the only thing you used to like about Christmas in the orphanage. The one time of the year when you could be guaranteed a piece of fresh fruit all to yourself. You used to take for ever, peeling it and slicing it to make it last, and all the other boys would be jealous, because they'd finished theirs. You said it was the most delicious thing you'd ever eaten and no fancy dessert you'd been served in the world's finest restaurants had ever come close to that taste.'

He sat back in his chair, his expression indecipherable in the flickering candlelight, though the note in his voice was one of surprise. 'I told you all that?'

'You talked about a lot of things in the early days, Giacomo. Less so as time went on.' She cleared her throat. 'Shall I go and fetch it—make sure you get your vitamin C for the day? I've fanned it out on the plate so it looks as pretty as a picture.'

But he shook his head impatiently. 'No. Let's go and sit by the fire. I want to talk to you and we may as well be comfortable.'

'Okay,' she said, trying to inject a brightness she wasn't really feeling. 'But I really do have masses to do, so let's try and keep it brief, shall we?'

His scowl indicated he wasn't used to working against the clock where women were concerned and Louise got up from the table to sink into the squashy depths of the sofa. Instinctively, she pressed her knees primly together as Giacomo put her wine glass down on a nearby table and sat down beside her.

'Tell me about our wedding,' he began, without preamble.

She nodded. 'What do you want to know?'

'Who was there?'

'Nobody connected to either of us. It was very small. We got two witnesses off the street.'

'Why?' His brow darkened. 'Was it supposed to be a secret?'

Louise felt a pain so intense that she nearly blurted it out then. But he had told her explicitly that he didn't want an information dump. They didn't have to talk about the baby. Not now. Maybe not ever. She was just acceding to his wishes, she told herself woodenly. It wasn't a question of cowardice. 'It was discreet, rather than secret. You said if the press got wind of it, they would be all over it like a rash and it was better not to make a big announcement. You told me you were afraid your lifestyle might overwhelm me and you didn't want to throw me in at the deep end, so you would introduce me to Milanese society gradually, but that never really happened and I thought...'

'What?' he prompted as her words tailed off. 'What did you think, Louise?'

His words were so soft and unusually probing that she found herself opening up to him in a way she'd never done before. 'I th-thought you were ashamed of me,' she said, not quite able to iron out the sudden wobble in her voice. 'You said yourself the other day that I wasn't what you were expecting. I was a very ordinary woman you had plucked from obscurity and you were a global superstar billionaire. Maybe we were a mismatch—our worlds were so far apart.'

'But you knew that where I started in life was

very different from the place where I ended up,' he argued. 'My mother died when I was eleven and I never knew my father. You can't get a much more basic beginning than a boy who left the orphanage and started working in a metal factory at the age of fourteen.'

'But you saw potential in that factory and exploited it, Giacomo,' she argued. 'You told me about all the poor older people in your neighbourhood who couldn't afford glasses and how you persuaded your boss to let you make some in your spare time. Nobody could have foreseen how that simple act would take off. That you would find that magical gap in the market which every entrepreneur seeks, or that you'd end up owning so many global brands which rake in an absolute fortune. Not many orphaned boys of fourteen do that,' she added drily.

He smiled. 'True.'

Louise put her glass down on the table beside her, reminding herself to beware of the power of that arrogantly sexy smile. 'Would you like to see a photo? Of our wedding?'

'You have one?'

'On my phone.' In a way it was a relief to be able to move away from the distraction of his closeness, though what she really wanted to do was snuggle up and get even closer. She rose and went to where she'd left it on the mantelpiece, aware of standing on unfa-

miliarly high heels as she flicked through the album
and found what she was looking for. She walked back
over to the sofa, glancing down at the raven gleam
of his hair and the broad set of his shoulders, which
were covered in the softest silk. Her fingers weren't
quite steady as she handed him the phone and sank
down next to him again. 'Here.'

He took it from her and studied it in silence for
a long moment. What did he make of it? she wondered. She hadn't allowed herself to look at it for a
long time—telling herself it was a pointless exercise
to keep rehashing the past if she wanted to move
on. She had tried to convince herself that it was a
single shot of a couple who should never have been
married. But now, all she could see was a radiant
happiness and excitement on the faces of the newly-
weds, certainly on hers—and very possibly on his.
He looked younger and more carefree—even though
it wasn't really that long ago. Could he see that, too,
or did he think it was just the camera playing tricks?
A captured moment, frozen in time, allowing for
many different interpretations, depending on who
was looking at it.

'Your parents?' he questioned suddenly. 'Why
weren't they there?'

'Because they died when I was a child,' she explained softly, before being bold enough to add,

'Actually, our parentless state was one of the few things we had in common.'

His jaw tightened. 'So you don't have any relatives?'

'Just the one. My aunt, who brought me up after they died.'

'But she wasn't there to see you get married?'

'No, though I didn't actually invite her. As I said, it wasn't that kind of wedding. And anyway...' Louise gave a short laugh '...she isn't really into celebrations.'

Because Aunt Maeve was one of life's disapprovers. She had disapproved of her younger sister, Louise's mother, and of the man she had married—and by default of the frightened little girl who had been turned over to her care after the tragic drowning of her parents. She had done her best for her niece, but her actions had been inspired by duty rather than love. Maybe that was where she had gone so wrong, Louise thought. Because if you were unfamiliar with the concept of love, mightn't you go looking for it in all the wrong places?

Giacomo had done the same as her aunt, she recognised suddenly. He had married her out of duty, because she had been carrying his child. Love had never really entered the equation, even though she'd been desperate to believe in it at the time.

'Did I ever meet her?' he questioned.

Louise picked up her glass of Bardolino and took a sip of the rich red wine. 'Once.'

'Did she like me?'

She looked him straight in the eye, a reluctant smile playing around her lips. 'I believe that's what they call a loaded question. Do you really want me to answer?'

'Of course.' He shrugged and gave the flicker of a responding smile. 'My skin, as I believe you say, is thick.'

'She said she could see exactly why I had fallen for you...'

'But?'

She put her glass down and when she glanced up, she had to steel herself against the ravaged beauty of his face. 'She said it would never last. She said we were too different and our worlds were miles apart. And she was right.'

'Was she always so negative?'

'Always.'

'And what happened to your parents?' he questioned. 'Tell me about them.'

'My mother was a dancer—'

'Ah. That would explain your legs.'

She wanted to remonstrate with him for an interruption which was making her body spring to instant life, and she wanted to purr with pleasure all at the same time. She shot him a warning look. 'Do you want the story, or not?'

'Yes.'

'My father was an actor. Both small-time. Both only moderately talented in a notoriously competitive field, which meant, of course, that they never got much work. They ended up working on cruise ships—my dad as a croupier and my mum in the chorus line. Apparently, they liked it. It meant they could see the world and convince themselves they'd made a success in their chosen careers—and it meant they had zero responsibilities. They weren't into responsibility.' She sighed. 'And then one day I came along and threw a spanner in the works, because having a child didn't really fit into the life they had, or the life they had planned.'

'So what happened?'

She shrugged. 'I only know what my aunt told me. She said my mum left the ship to look after me, only she wasn't really happy. She spent her whole time fretting about my dad and wondering what he was doing when she wasn't there. And then one time when he was home on leave, they went drinking in Southampton to celebrate. It was a foul night and for some reason, they decided to go for a walk along the water. They must have fallen in, and drowned, though they didn't find their bodies for several days.'

She swallowed. 'A terrible death and yet a very mundane death, all at the same time.'

'I'm sorry,' he said.

She thought he was about to reach out his hand to take hers and, in an attempt to stop him, Louise picked up her wine glass again, though she didn't drink from it. She didn't think she could take being comforted or cajoled by that soft note of compassion in his voice right now. It might make her start imagining all the things she liked about him and wanted from him—and she was never going to get them.

'It meant my aunt got custody of me,' she continued staunchly. 'Something I don't think she was prepared or equipped for. She was quite strict and religious and a bit of a slavedriver. In return for my board and lodgings, I did most of the housework. She said she would support me until I was sixteen and after that, I was on my own.'

It had been a joyless upbringing but she must have inherited something of her parents' acting ability because she had always hidden behind a cheery expression. That had been one of the things which had made her such a popular choice as a waitress. It had been a loveless upbringing, too—which might go some way to explaining why she'd fallen head over heels for the first and only man she'd had sex with. 'I did very well at school because I worked hard, but I didn't go to college. I left school at sixteen as planned,' she finished flatly, easing her feet out of her high-heeled shoes almost without thinking about it. 'But I discovered that I had cultivated exactly the kind of skills which the world of catering was crying out for. I could cook and clean and serve someone a cup of tea without spilling it.'

'Did I know any of this?' he demanded.

She nodded. 'Some of it. Not all—and not in quite so much detail. Like I said, we didn't really go in for a lot of conversation and you had a rather short attention span in those days.'

Giacomo sucked in a sharp breath as he heard the sadness in her voice, which she was trying very hard to hide, and somehow that affected him in a way he wasn't expecting. 'Was I a terrible husband?' he questioned suddenly.

There was silence for a moment as she met his gaze with a look of mockery. 'That's not a fair question, Giacomo. You told me you wanted me to be objective. How is going over your perceived faults going to help get your memory back?'

It was prevarication, yes—but in a way, this was exactly what he wanted to hear. Giacomo could think of things he'd much rather do than analyse his suitability as a husband, especially when she was looking at him like that. The tremble of her lips and the darkening of her eyes felt too much like temptation. Way too much for him to resist. Because when a man was presented with such alluring invitation written in her extraordinary eyes, what else was he going to do but act on it?

'I know one thing which might.' He put his hands on her arms and still she looked at him that way. As if she needed this as much as he did. And hadn't he resisted the urge to kiss her earlier, even though he'd known that she'd wanted him to?

Why had he done that?

To test his resolve and demonstrate his steely control? To prove he could do without what he most wanted—which was sex? Or to show Louise that she must expect nothing from him, other than a generous pay cheque and a speedy divorce? Either way it didn't matter because she was here now and they both knew where the boundaries lay—and if they crossed them, so what? It was only ever going to be temporary.

But Giacomo couldn't stem his low moan of hunger as he pulled her into his arms to kiss her and instantly she opened her lips to greet him. He felt the wild beat of anticipation, because how good was it to enjoy the slick lace of their tongues and hear her sigh of pleasure when he slipped his inside her mouth? He was ready to feast on her. To touch and smell her. He wanted to be inside her. Thrusting long and deep and hard and then spilling his seed until he was empty and dry. But for now, this kiss would have to do.

His arms snaked around her back as if he were afraid she might just disappear—as if what was happening was as unreliable as his memory and he needed to cling to whatever was available to him—and suddenly she felt *very* available. She was so tiny. So pliable. He could feel the soft weight of her breasts pressing against him and the rocky thrust of her nipples, and suddenly he knew exactly what they would look like. Small and rosy—with bullet-like little tips. It was a revelation. It wasn't the memory he had been seeking but it was the one he got. A sensual trigger to his already overheated blood.

Hot fire raged through him. He could have ripped the clothes from her body, knowing she would be wet and ready for him. He could have pushed her down and entered her from behind and she would have given nothing but an appreciative moan as she tilted her bottom to accommodate him. Because on some subliminal level he recognised that intimacy with her had always been different than with anyone else. He thought of the way he had looked in that snatched wedding photo and had seen someone he hadn't recognised. It had come as a shock to see how relaxed and almost *happy* he'd appeared in that picture and he wondered if his amnesia was making him unduly nostalgic. Or was he just refusing to confront the reality of what life with Louise had really been like?

He got some intimation then of her power over

him. Of her ability to dissolve him, or perhaps to destroy him, by making his legendary control slip away.

Wasn't that too high a price to pay for the fleeting pleasures of sex?

Warnings flashed like fireworks in his mind, telling him to go about this in a more measured way, but he was too eaten up by desire to heed them. Hungrily, she kissed him back as he reached behind to unzip her dress—and he, who had never fumbled in his life, was suddenly behaving like a novice, his fingers were shaking so much. The velvet parted as he slid down the zip and the flesh of her back felt smooth and soft beneath his fingers. Like a ripe nectarine. He tugged the bodice down and tore his mouth away from hers to observe the delicious vision she presented. Those heaving globes—their creamy weight straining against a black bra which appeared to be at least one size too small. She was staring up at him, her eyes dark and liquid with lust, strands of glossy hair tumbling down around her face. She looked like a study in decadence. She looked like the most beautiful thing he'd ever seen.

'Not here,' he bit out.

Her breathing was unsteady as she gasped out her response. 'Aren't you making a bit of an assumption?'

'No games, Louise,' he warned her. 'Not tonight. Do you want this as much as I do?'

'Of…of course I do,' she said unsteadily, before shooting an anxious glance at the debris-covered dining table. 'But, look… I've still got all the clearing up to do.'

He didn't even bother to answer her absurd statement, just scooped her up in his arms and carried her towards the staircase, filled with a sense of masterful possession.

'Where are you taking me?'

He stared down at her face where her eyes looked so wide and dark. 'You know damned well where I'm taking you. You can change your mind any time you like,' he ground out. 'But tell me in this moment that you don't want to go to bed with me, Louise, and I will call you a liar.'

CHAPTER EIGHT

WITH HIS HANDS firmly underneath her bottom, Louise felt as if she'd lost all touch with reality as Giacomo carried her up the sweeping staircase of his ancient home and kicked open the door of the master bedroom. He must have lit the fire before he'd come down to dinner, because the room was deliciously warm and light from the flames was dancing in flickering patterns across the ceiling and onto the silk rugs. Splashing like liquid gold over the coverlet of the vast bed, which she had made that very morning.

She wasn't supposed to be here. Just as she wasn't supposed to be letting him place her on the soft mattress and then bend his head to her breast, to suck at a thrusting nipple with the teasing graze of his teeth, which she was certain was going to rupture the delicate lace of her bra. She shouldn't be lying here with her dress rucked up to her waist. She should be down in the kitchen clearing up, before doing some last-minute prep for tomorrow's meal. Peeling sprouts or putting the mince pies in the oven.

The mince pies...

But her to-do list slid from Louise's thoughts as sexual hunger took precedence over everything, even the common sense which she had clung to like a lifeline during the long months of her separation from Giacomo. Her body was hungry for him—and if she concentrated on *that* need rather than the useless longing for something deeper, then what harm could this do? He wanted her and she wanted him and they were still married. Why not? And Giacomo had taught her this, she recognised achingly. He had taught her to enjoy her body—and his. He had somehow managed to eradicate the indoctrination of the over-strict aunt who had reared her. He had taught her that consensual sex could never be considered a sin.

Her head tipped back to accommodate his seeking lips as they roved over her neck, her eyelids fluttering to a close as he peeled the dress down over her hips and pushed it off her completely. She felt the rush of air to her heated skin and opened her eyes again to see him staring at her with a look which was midway between incredulity and smoky desire.

'Did you intend for this to happen? Is that why you are dressed like *this*…?' he demanded, one quivering fingertip tracing the fine edge of her black hold-up stockings before drifting upwards to touch the silky outline of her black thong panties.

She sucked in a breath as his finger found the taut gusset of her damp panties and recognised how close she was to the edge already. How could she have gone for eighteen months without any intimacy at all and then be poised on the brink of orgasm so quickly? It was like one of those sports cars which went from nought to sixty in three seconds…

Her reply sounded slurred and husky as she tried to formulate her skewed thoughts into some kind of order. 'Believe it or not, but my everyday underwear doesn't exactly *go* with a dress like…' Like the one you've just hurled to the floor, she wanted to say— but he was tearing off his silk shirt, seemingly uncaring about the buttons which were popping off in the process.

She'd never seen him like this before. His eyes were blazing black fire, his sensual lips parted as if he were having difficulty drawing in each ragged breath. He had always been the perfect lover— always ensuring that she had more orgasms than she'd considered possible, before addressing his own needs. She had only ever known him as measured— his steely restraint always conquering his rampant desire, until *he* was ready to release it. He was the master and she the complete novice, and in terms of experience they were worlds apart. She had never imagined he could be so out of control.

He slid his hand around her back to free her bra and remove it, so that it fluttered to the floor in a crumple of black lace. He sucked in a low breath of appreciation as her swollen breasts came tumbling out. She could feel them jiggle, unfettered and free, as his gaze roved over them and it felt so good to be bathed in that fierce ebony light. Dangerously good. A whisper of warning trickled over her skin. Because where was this going to leave her?

'Giacomo—'

'I don't want to talk,' he growled. 'Just tell me, yes or no. Do you want me to stop?'

Yes, shouted the voice inside her head. 'No,' she whispered back.

'Voglio soltanto,' he grated as he dug his fingers into the mussed mass of her hair. 'I…just…want… to…'

But whatever he had been about to say was lost in translation as his mouth fastened itself around her nipple and he sucked long and hard, causing darts of exquisite pleasure to arrow through her receptive body, so that she made a mewling little sound—like a kitten.

And, God forgive her, but she began to touch him back. She undid his belt and, with far less dexterity than he had displayed, began scrabbling ineffectu-

ally with the zip as she tried to remove his trousers.
Her impatience seemed at first to amuse him and
then he pushed her hand away and dealt with the garment himself, until all he was wearing was a pair of
black boxer shorts.

There was a question in his eyes as his gaze swept
over her, but she must have silently answered it because he began to peel off her black silk stockings,
managing to make her feel even more decadent in
the process—something she hadn't thought possible.
Next came her thong panties and although she was
longing for him to graze his finger over her exquisitely aroused nub, he didn't—just gave a little moan
and told her he was having difficulty pacing himself.
Did she convey some of her frustration to him? Was
he aware—as she was—that the way he was responding to her was uncharacteristic? She'd never heard
him admit to not being in total control before. Perhaps that was why he gave a soft laugh, lifting the
panties to his nostrils and inhaling deeply—before
tossing them aside to join her discarded bra.

Boldly, she peeled off his boxer shorts, caressing the hard, silken globes of his buttocks as he
reached between her legs, his fingers brushing over
the velvety wet folds. Something about the way he
was looking at her was making her feel like nothing
more than a sexual being, but that wasn't enough to
stop her right then. She didn't think anything could

have stopped what was happening to her. She quivered as he stroked her and writhed her bare bottom against the under-sheet which she had tugged smooth that very morning.

Rapidly, the pleasure built—layer by incredible layer—until she didn't think she could take any more. He gave a low laugh as she reached the peak and then she was calling out his name as she pulsed around his finger, swamped by abandon as she tumbled over the edge. She was aware that he was watching her, as her orgasm shimmered to a dreamy end and that was when Louise knew she had to act—and act quickly. She saw his brief look of surprise as she pushed him back against the bank of pillows, instead of spreading her legs wide to accommodate the hard push of his erection, as usually she would have done.

'Louise,' he groaned, as she captured his shaft between her thumb and forefinger.

She had never heard him sound quite so helpless as she flicked her hand up and down over his rocky length, with a lightness and precision which he had taught her. His eyes were closed now, a look of naked bliss contorting his scarred yet still beautiful features. She felt the tension in him grow, his hard limbs growing tense, his hands bunching into fists, and she took him in her mouth just before he came, his fingers tangled in her hair as he ground out something incomprehensible in his native tongue before spurting his seed inside her mouth.

She lay there afterwards, her tongue exploring the roof of her mouth as she tasted the essence of him, her head resting dreamily against his chest. The moment felt so perfect and complete that she wished she could just be magicked out of his bed, to find herself safely tucked up on that monastic mattress upstairs. Safe in a place where there would be no questions or discussions to spoil the memory of what had just happened. But life was never that easy, and after a few minutes of silence, Giacomo stirred, levering himself up and rolling across the bed so that he was facing her, and she didn't avert her eyes quickly enough not to notice the stir of a new erection at his groin.

But for all his problems with communication, nobody could ever have accused Giacomo of not understanding the language of the body—and he had always instinctively known what her physical needs were. His eyes were narrowed, his ebony gaze searching as it swept over her with laser-like intensity.

'You don't want to have full sex?'

It was a perceptive yet brutal statement and she wished he had put it another way—but how? It wasn't the kind of subject you could soften or make sound romantic, was it? He couldn't know that the thought of penetration horrified her—and not just because she was terrified of getting pregnant again. She was scared of the emotional impact of having Giacomo inside her again. Because in Louise's limited experience, sex had a power all of its own. It made you feel ridiculously close to a man. As if you were one person instead of two.

And that was nothing but an illusion.

It always had been.

'No.' She bit her lip. 'No, I don't.'

He propped himself up onto one elbow, his black eyes glittering as they swept over her. 'Do you want to tell me why not?'

His words were too forensic. Too bald. Louise shook her head. 'Not really.'

'Are you sure?'

If she hadn't known better, she might have thought she detected a whisper of understanding in Giacomo's voice, but that was nothing but wishful thinking. And not only was it stupid, it was also completely irrelevant at this stage in their relationship. There was no room in her life for romantic yearnings. No place for what-ifs. She had to be pragmatic—about the present *and* the future. She was here for a couple more days and she would be a self-deluding fool if she believed that they weren't going to end up in a similar position again. The sexual chemistry between them was too potent to believe it was just going to fizzle out and go away, and she wasn't deluded enough to deny that she wanted more of *this*. There was nothing fundamentally wrong with seeking pleasure, she decided, but this, too, had to be on her terms.

'Okay, I'll tell you why.'

He propped himself up on one muscular forearm, his dark eyebrows raised in question.

'It's too intimate,' she said truthfully and then ventured further than she had intended to go. 'And I think it would be too sad.'

'Too sad?' he echoed.

'It will muddle my head.' She shrugged, not caring that her breasts were bare, but then she had always felt unbelievably relaxed when naked with Giacomo. And that was another reason why she needed to blurt out these next words before his powerful charisma wrapped itself around her like a silken cord and obliterated all her doubts and fears. 'It will make it hard for me to remember where we are right now, which is poised on the brink of divorce.' She forced a smile. 'Which I think is my cue to go upstairs to my own room.'

He didn't respond to this—though, to be fair, neither did she. She certainly didn't act on her intention to move. She told herself she was still sated from her orgasm and feeling lazy—and it was just too warm and comfortable here, with Giacomo beside her. His body was almost touching her, though not quite—but even so, she could feel the heat which radiated from his powerful frame. She thought how bizarre it was that they could lie there in companionable silence, even though their marriage was heading for the buffers. And wasn't there a bit of her which wanted to hold on to this moment, which was the closest she'd come to contentment in a long time?

After a moment or two, he reached out to touch her hair and Louise didn't stop him as he began to stroke it as he'd always done back in the day, enjoying the soft, rhythmic action of his fingers. She felt a slow warmth begin to creep over her as her skin began to glow. And not just her skin. Her breasts had started to tingle again and she could feel a molten tug deep inside her. It was the renewed blossoming of desire and she wondered afterwards what might have happened next, had his next words not shattered the unusual sense of peace and sent it hurtling into the stratosphere.

'You were a virgin when we first met,' he said slowly.

It was a statement, not a question, and her mouth dried. 'You've just remembered?'

He captured a thick strand of hair and wound it around his finger. 'In a way.'

She could feel the flicker of fear and realised how much she wanted to cling to the present, rather than

go back to the bitter landscape of the past. 'How...
how much?'

His splintered jet eyes grew thoughtful. 'We went
to your little apartment. I remember the background
noise of planes.'

'Very close to the airport. That's why it was so
affordable,' she interjected flippantly.

But he carried on as if she hadn't spoken. 'I think
I'd started to guess you were an innocent by the time
we were in bed, and I offered to stop.' There was a
pause and suddenly his face darkened and his expression became almost pained. 'I'm asking you again.
Did I take advantage of you, Louise?'

'How?' she challenged. 'You think you were
the only man to have ever made a pass at me, Giacomo? You think I was incapable of knowing my
own mind—or knowing what it was I wanted?'

'No. You certainly knew what it was you wanted.
You were so small and so determined. So fierce...
You wrapped your arms around my back and told me
you couldn't bear to stop.' His voice became thick.
'So we didn't.'

Something about the way he was speaking—
which was unlike any way she'd ever heard him
speak before—made Louise instinctively reach out
for him. She put her arms around him, but this time
her fingers met the ridged scars which criss-crossed
his back, rather than the smooth expanse of old.

'Not pretty, are they?' he questioned acidly.

Slowly, she slid her fingers over each one, real-ising he probably *had* deliberately drawn her atten-tion to them when she'd seen him half naked on the corridor earlier. 'People are drawn to imperfection,' she said slowly. 'It's much more interesting. I mean, a shop-bought cake looks perfect on the outside—but put one next to a slightly lopsided home-made ver-sion and I know which one will sell first.'

He smiled. 'I've been compared to many things in my life, Louise,' he observed drily. 'But never a cake.'

She found herself wishing he hadn't done that, because the curve of his mouth looked so gorgeous. And so unbelievably kissable. This was getting more addictive by the second and Louise knew exactly what she should do. 'I ought to go,' she mumbled, reluctantly letting her hands fall.

But he shook his dark head. 'You don't have to go anywhere. Close your eyes. The lids look heavy. Heavy as lead. Go on, close them.'

Had he recently undergone a course in hypno-sis? wondered Louise, with sleepy suspicion. But she must have been more tired or more affected by the rush of endorphins than she'd imagined, because the next time she slitted open her eyes it wasn't to see a night-time room, splashed golden by firelight. The fire had long since gone out and there was nothing but grey ash in the grate. She blinked against the strangely bright light which was streaming in through the windows.

She held her breath, not daring to move. The room *felt* empty and she was pretty sure Giacomo wasn't in bed with her. She risked turning her head to one side, unable to decide whether it was relief or disappointment she felt when she saw that the enormous bed was definitely empty, save for her.

She lay back against the pillows and thought about what she had done. And what he had done. What they had said and how she had reacted. She knew that her actions hadn't just been completely reckless—they were potentially risky. She had thrown caution to the wind by having sexual contact with her estranged husband in a very deliberate way, and now her feelings towards him were no longer quite so black and white. She sighed. Or maybe she was just kidding herself, because since when had her feelings for Giacomo been that straightforward?

So where *was* he?

She looked around the vast room. The red velvet dress from her past life had been retrieved from the floor and now lay draped neatly over the back of a chair by the wardrobe. Alongside it were her discarded underwear and a pair of filmy black stockings. She supposed she could put on the wildly inappropriate morning outfit and creep back along the creaky corridors and head upstairs, hoping he wouldn't hear her before she reached her room.

Or she could brazen it out and borrow something of Giacomo's to wear. Why not? Wasn't that one of the unwritten privileges of being a man's lover, even if it was only temporary?

She hunted around and found one of his sweaters—an old one which she recognised—and *that* made her feel peculiar as she pulled it on over her head. In softest cashmere and the colour of an inky sky, it came to mid-thigh and enveloped her with his scent.

His scent.

His gorgeous scent.

She closed her eyes. She didn't *want* to feel a stab of longing when she thought about him, just as she didn't want to feel a dull ache at the thought that this was all going to end very soon, but she guessed that was her punishment for having let him seduce her last night.

She didn't have a clue what the time was because she'd left her phone downstairs, but as she padded barefoot over to the window she let out a gasp of surprise—because didn't snow always come as a surprise, even if you knew it was on the way?

It was magical.

Overnight, the world had been clothed in white. A thick, glittering mantle covering the trees and rolling parkland and explaining why the light seemed super-naturally bright. It looked like a fairy tale—like one of those animated cards you sometimes saw on the Internet. It made Louise's spirits lift with an inexplicable kind of joy, and surely that was dangerous, too.

She turned away from the snowy scene and thought about the day ahead.

So now what?

CHAPTER NINE

THE SHOWER NEXT to the servant's bedroom didn't provide what Louise was looking for—which was a powerful stream of water to wash away the scent and memories of what had happened the night before. The cubicle wasn't the largest in the world, but she made the best of it before sliding into her uniform, because that seemed the best way of putting in place the barriers which she and her estranged husband had torn down in some style last night.

She went in search of Giacomo, who she found in—of all places—the kitchen. A kitchen she barely recognised with its gleaming and tidy surfaces. She blinked. Where was all the debris from last night's meal? The unwashed pots and jugs and measuring spoons. The bag of flour and sticky egg whisk? All the stuff she'd neglected to clear up because Giacomo had carried her up to his bed, leaving chaos behind?

In the coffee-scented warmth, he was standing

with his back to her—black hair curling over the back of a soft sweater, close-cut jeans emphasising his narrow hips and the powerful shanks of his thighs. A shaft of longing arrowed through her. Now *why* had she suddenly started remembering the hair-roughened flesh of his lower belly and the way she had trickled her fingers down over the rippled flesh to find the hard nudge of his erection, before clamping her mouth round it? Communication was going to be difficult enough this morning without indulging in distracting erotic recall, and throwing a rapidly emerging desire into the mix. She wondered whether either of them would have the nerve to confront the elephant which was preparing to charge into the room. Did they ignore the fact that last night they had indulged in a blissful kind of nearly-there sex, or pretend it had never happened?

'So. Have I left it long enough?' he drawled, still with his back to her.

The unexpected question startled Louise out of her introspection. 'Long enough for...what?'

He turned round and she almost wished he hadn't, because it was easier to address him impartially when he wasn't observing her—less so when those black eyes were piercing through her and making her skin shiver in response. He had obviously showered and changed but he hadn't bothered shaving and the dark shadow around his chiselled jaw added an extra layer of danger and intimacy, which Louise could have done without.

'For you to study me and work out what we're going to say about what happened last night.'

'I suppose this morning-after scene is hugely familiar to you.' She raised her eyebrows. 'Unless you're a mind-reader, or something?'

'It's a big no to the first part of your statement and a possible yes to the second—certainly where you are concerned.' He threw her a look of cool challenge. 'So I'm right?'

'Of course you are.' Louise sighed. They had agreed to be honest. They had been extremely close last night. What was the point of being coy? 'None of that stuff last night was supposed to happen—'

'Stuff?' he echoed, a faint smile playing around the edges of his lips.

'That's right,' she continued stolidly. 'And inevitably, it's going to feel a bit...*awkward*.'

'Sit down.' He indicated a machine which resembled a small spacecraft. 'And I'll make you some coffee.'

'That's supposed to be my job.' But she sat down anyway, because her knees had started feeling weak when he looked at her that way. 'What are you even doing in here? It's like finding a lion in a tearoom. Are you responsible for the incredibly tidy state of the kitchen?'

'What else did you think had happened to it?' His gaze was mocking. 'That a fleet of unseen servants stole in while we were sleeping? And now you're blushing, which is both unexpected and very charming. I think I'd better make you some breakfast, don't you?'

'Breakfast?'

'You know? The meal you eat first thing in the morning, or in this case...' he gave a swift glance at the gold timepiece which gleamed at his wrist '...nearly midday, so I guess we'll have to call it brunch.'

Louise blinked in astonishment, aware that she still hadn't looked at her phone—and she couldn't remember the last time she'd done *that*. 'Did I really sleep that long?'

'It seems so.'

'Where—?'

His dark eyebrows shot up. 'Did I sleep?'

'You're mind-reading again, Giacomo. Much more of that and we'll have to buy you a crystal ball and hire you out for summer fetes.'

He smiled. 'I slept in the room next door, because I got the distinct feeling you wanted to be on your own.'

She wanted to tell him not to smile like that and certainly not to be so thoughtful. To tell him that was the kind of considerate gesture which made a woman read far too much into a situation and she was in danger of doing exactly that.

So stop flirting with him.

Stop wishing he'd put that wretched coffee capsule down and come over here and kiss her with the same hungry passion he'd displayed last night. Because somehow, despite her determination to dismiss what had happened as a big mistake, she couldn't bear to think that their single sexual encounter might have proved conclusive. Had that perfunctory display of mutual pleasure extinguished all his desire for her—and if that were the case, wasn't it a good thing they would soon be heading for the divorce courts?

'You were right, I did,' she mumbled. 'Thanks.'

'You're welcome.' The machine made a couple of steaming emissions and he pushed a cup of coffee towards her, followed by a small jug. 'No sugar, am I right?'

She added a splash of milk. 'You're remembering other stuff?'

'Little things, here and there.' He poured a coffee for himself and dropped a sugar cube into the inky brew. 'As you said the other day—inconsequential things which mean nothing but which, when taken as a whole, begin to form a solid picture.'

Louise sipped her coffee—which was very good—unable to shake off her fears about his memory returning and not just because she knew some of the things which were lying in wait for him. Things which had the potential to hurt her all over again and take her back to that helpless, hopeless place she'd dreaded returning to. Should she tell him? Blurt it all out and replace this precarious sense of ease with the most heartbreaking memory of all? But how could she do that—and on Christmas Day when, for a brief moment, he seemed almost...contented? She took another sip of coffee. No. She would wait until *he* remembered—which he had insisted on doing from the outset.

Coward, mocked a voice in her head, but she pushed the thought away as she watched him making toast, realising that they'd never shared this kind of domestic intimacy when they'd been married.

'Eggs?' he questioned.

'Great.' Louise put her cup down. 'Though I wasn't aware that you actually knew *how* to cook.'

'Alpha men don't cook?' he challenged. 'Is that what you're implying?'

'Something like that. You always had servants when we were together.'

He looked up from breaking a fifth egg into a bowl, but now his voice was edged with a hint of steel. 'You think that a boy from the orphanage doesn't learn how to fend for himself?'

'I don't know.' She hesitated. 'I only know the bare facts. You never used to want to talk about it.

You just said it was a big, grim place and the best thing about it was the day you were able to leave.'

Giacomo nodded as he beat the eggs and added them to the butter which was sizzling in the pan, acknowledging that what she said was true. Because keeping things to himself had been his default mechanism. The less people knew, the less hold or influence they would have over him. And isolation was power. It was all he had really ever known. Why deviate from a path which had guided him so successfully throughout his life? 'And nothing about that has changed,' he said coldly. 'Why would I want to talk about an experience which is best forgotten?'

Giacomo saw the unmistakable disappointment which clouded her eyes as he pushed a plate of eggs towards her, but she quickly turned her head as she reached for the toast. She looked very different this morning—almost unrecognisable from the temptress of last night in her scarlet dress, high heels and the star necklace. He had been surprised and a little disappointed when she had appeared in uniform, because it suggested she was eager to put the relationship firmly back on a professional footing. And hadn't he revelled in the distinctly *unprofessional* outcome which had ended their evening?

Yet he thought how beautiful she looked, sitting at the wooden table in her pink shirt, with her glossy dark hair piled up in that very sexy updo.

Her cheeks were rosy and so were her lips as she munched hungrily on a piece of toast and she gave the appearance of a woman who had been thoroughly ravished, though of course, she hadn't—not quite. He wondered how she would react if he told her that he hadn't gone straight off to one of the other rooms last night. That he'd lain there for a while, watching as she slept, unwilling to walk away from the unusual sense of warmth which had stolen over his skin as he had watched the rising and falling of her magnificent breasts.

He had known that if he had reached for her—in those soft early hours dominated by the senses rather than by reason—then she would have been back in his arms. Her lips would have reached blindly for his in the darkness and who knew what might have happened? Actually, he knew very well what would have happened—the chemistry between them was way too powerful to resist a scenario like that.

But he didn't want to possess her like that, by default. He wanted her *telling* him she wanted him. He wanted her alert and hungry, not half drugged by sleep. His mouth hardened. Was sex the way to fire up his memory? A gut-deep feeling inside him suggested that everything would come flooding back the moment he entered her. Or was that simply his body's way of justifying his urgent need to possess her again?

The ache in his groin was distracting and he ate his brunch mechanically while Louise focussed her attention on her eggs—taking an extraordinarily long time about it, as if she found eating easier than talking. But when she could legitimately dawdle no longer and had pushed her plate away, he sat back in his chair and studied her.

'Shall we go for a walk?' he questioned. 'In the snow?'

Startled, she glanced out of the window, as if she had just been reminded of the white world which lay beyond the window.

'What...now?'

'Why not?'

'I'll give you one very good reason.' She indicated the untidy breakfast table between them. 'There's this to sort out. And more.'

'Forget it,' he growled.

'I can't forget it, Giacomo. You're paying me to be your housekeeper and it would be a dereliction of duty for me to just waltz off and leave the place looking a tip, like I did last night.' She pursed her lips together with a look of self-censure. 'Don't they say that once is a mistake, but twice is a pattern?'

'So you think last night was a mistake, do you, Louise?'

Her cheeks went very pink and it was a moment or two before she nodded. 'I'm certain of it.'

'But you enjoyed it.'

She looked at him with appeal in her eyes. 'Of course I did. But that doesn't make it right.'

But he hardened his heart against the plea for understanding in her eyes, because he wanted this. He wanted it very badly. And so did she, if she was being honest. 'If you want to talk about duty, that's fine,' he said coolly. 'But as your employer, I really ought to be the one to decide how you spend your time. And right now, I want you to come walking in the snow with me.'

'So it's an order, rather than a suggestion?'

'If that makes it more acceptable for you, *sì*.'

Had she always been so cautious around him? he wondered. Had those extraordinary eyes always grown wary, as if everything he said needed to be examined for possible damage limitation? He frowned. Had he been a difficult man to live with? And if that was the case, maybe he should cut her some slack.

But to his surprise, she smiled and nodded her agreement and once again, Giacomo was unprepared for the impact of that smile. It was like the sun flickering through the dense mist of a morning fog and making everything grow clear. He felt the stab of pain somewhere deep inside him and he didn't like it. Because he recognised that this was emotional pain and it was too like the stuff he'd grown up with.

Hadn't he spent his life avoiding feeling that way again?

Running away, taunted a voice in his head, but he pushed it away with a finality born of grinding habit.

'Okay,' she agreed. 'In that case, I'll go and get changed into something more suitable.'

She was back ten minutes later, wearing jeans and the fur-trimmed anorak, her shiny hair loose and spilling down over her shoulders.

He shot her a questioning look. 'Wasn't there something else you could have worn?'

'Of course there was,' she answered coolly. 'A cashmere coat which probably cost the equivalent of a year's wages and a very rakish wide-brimmed hat. *Very* billionaire's wife. But that's not me, is it, Giacomo? Not any more. This is me. Take it or leave it.'

Yet despite a fierce defence which was bordering on defiance, Louise wasn't as sure of herself as she sounded. Should she admit that she'd been tempted to dress up as Signora Volterra one more time, because the beautiful garments had been beckoning to her and it *was* Christmas Day? Until she reminded herself that she wasn't Giacomo's wife any more. And if she indulged in any kind of masquerade, that would only make her feel even more confused than she already did. Wouldn't it blur the boundaries between them even more?

Because right now she wasn't sure *who* she was

as she stepped out into the snowy grounds, with Giacomo by her side. It was as if she'd morphed into a hybrid of the woman she'd been before and the woman she was now. She felt curiously *alive*—in a way she hadn't done since she'd left the marriage. But that was just sex. It must be. And already she was in trouble. Dreading the completion of her time here, when Giacomo would fly back to Milan and she would drive her little car through the snow to Stanwell and they would wave goodbye—this time for ever.

How long would it take her to forget him this time?

They crunched their way through the thick snow, which was made luminously bright by the pale sun. At least the wintry scene was beautiful enough to momentarily distract her from Giacomo's dark, Italianate beauty—but she could only look at snow-covered trees and vast sweeps of white for so long before her attention began to stray… She risked a peep at his profile, thinking how indomitable he looked against the brilliant landscape, and it suddenly dawned on her what a fool she had been to agree to his insane proposition. Why had she come here at all? Had she really imagined she would be immune to his spellbinding magnetism? That she could allow her emotions to be compromised and then to walk away unscathed?

'It's gorgeous,' she breathed, trying to drag her thoughts back from the precipice of regret. Trying to sound like a normal person who happened to be walking around the beautiful snowy countryside on Christmas Day.

'Isn't it?' he agreed softly.

But he was looking at her—not his vast estate—and she wished he wouldn't, because that smoky slant of his eyes wasn't helping the sudden rocketing of her pulse.

'Why don't we walk down to the lake?' she suggested, with a briskness which suddenly felt imperative.

But the lake had gone. It had disappeared beneath a thick coating of white, only adding to Louise's feelings of disconnection as they trudged back through the snow towards the ancient house. It was as if everything about the landscape was different, but underneath the surface it was all exactly the same. Like them, she thought grimly. Just like them.

'We walked like this once before on Christmas Day, didn't we?' Giacomo questioned suddenly.

'Yes.' Her steps slowed. 'Yes, we did.'

'I was holding your hand,' he said slowly.

She felt vulnerable. She wanted to tell him to *stop doing this*, but she couldn't, of course she couldn't—because this was why she was here. And his words took Louise right back there. He hadn't wanted to let go of her and she'd felt protected and cherished as he'd wrapped his big palm around her gloved fingers. Safe and protected and very loved. Wasn't it stupid how a little thing like that could make her feel as if it were some big deal? As if hand-holding was somehow more significant than hot sex.

'Right, again. You were.'

'And I built you a snowman.'

Silently, she nodded. It hardly seemed credible now, but he had done just that. And naturally, being Giacomo, he had created the biggest and most magnificent snowman in the entire history of the world, or so she'd thought at the time. Though, to be honest, if he'd just slammed two pieces of coal into the front of an icy mound, she probably would have cooed ecstatically over it. 'Yes, you did. You spent about an hour doing it while I was in the house, and then you covered up my eyes and led me out here to see it. It *was* pretty amazing.'

There was a pause. 'Shall I build you another one?'

And the crazy thing was that his unexpected question made her want to melt. Was that because it mimicked the tenderness he'd shown before, such a long time ago? Part of her wanted to say, *yes, please*—but common sense stopped her just in time. Because any minute now and she would start imagining that they were in one of those cheesy Christmas films—the type which had picturesque flakes of snow tumbling from the sky and he would brush one from her cheek before slowly bending his head to kiss her. And they didn't do those kind of kisses. Not any more. The only kisses they shared were of the pre-sex variety.

'I've outgrown snowmen,' she said repressively, relieved when they reached the house, rapidly removing her anorak and shaking the snow off her boots as Giacomo shut the door behind them.

'Excuse me. I need to find my phone,' she said quickly, and as she walked into the dining room she was overcome by another wave of surprise. Because Giacomo must have cleared away in here, too—*and* lit the fire. The room was deliciously warm and the light from the flames was reflected in the baubles on the Christmas tree, making them seem brighter than the midday sun.

Her phone was still on the table beside the sofa and Louise had just slid it into the back pocket of her jeans when she turned and saw Giacomo standing in the doorway, watching her. She felt something potent and inevitable flow between them. A powerful force which could not be halted by logic or reason. Something imperceptible shifted and changed as he walked across the room towards her. He was standing in front of her now but his eyes were narrowed as they surveyed her, as if he were trying to focus on something he couldn't quite see.

'Louise?' he said, in a low voice.

It was one of those one-word questions with the potential to convey a multitude of meaning, but Louise knew exactly what it was he was asking. For a moment she couldn't speak, she was so overcome with an emotion she didn't dare define. 'Yes,' she whispered back. 'Yes.'

It was assent and desire tied up in one soft word and Giacomo felt his blood roar in his veins as he bent his head to kiss her. It felt like for ever since he had tasted the pleasure of her lips, which of course was a complete distortion because it was only a few short hours ago. Yet it felt as if last night had just whetted his appetite—or maybe reminded him of all the things he'd been missing, because his desire for her right now felt *off the scale*.

He skated his hands over her body, his palms lingering fractionally on the pert thrust of her breasts, and she gave a breathless little moan in response. He cupped one heavy globe, feeling it peak as it strained towards him against the softness of her sweater. He felt her squirm and knew he had to get her horizontal as quickly as possible, yet the hardness at his groin was already so intense that he didn't trust himself to take her upstairs as he'd managed to do last night. He wanted her now. Here. In front of the flickering fire which was bathing the room in sunset colours. They'd made love here before, he realised. More than once.

Hunger flared through him as he eased her down onto the silken rug and sank down beside her, peeling off her sweater so that her lace-clad breasts burst free. He unclipped her bra and gave himself over to the highly pleasurable activity of licking the soft and abundant flesh until she was moaning with what sounded like a mixture of frustration and encouragement. And that was when he unzipped her jeans, tracing the tremble of his fingertips over the faint swell of her stomach.

'Help me,' he said urgently.

Louise thought she'd never known the man she married sound quite so helpless and she lifted her bottom to assist him with the removal of her jeans. She wondered if he'd noticed that she'd gone back to her Louise Greening underwear rather than the decadent lingerie she'd worn last night. But he didn't seem at all bothered as he hooked his fingers into the sides of her sensible panties and slid them down over her knees before flinging them aside so that they landed in a heap at the base of the dining table. She closed her eyes and briefly wondered what her boss at Posh Catering might have to say about *that*.

'Oh…' She quivered as he pushed her thighs apart and she thought—prayed—he was going to strum her badly aching bud with his finger. But no. He was bending his head towards her, his mouth finding the most private part of her—kissing and exploring the quivering molten core before delving his tongue into her wet heat.

He took his time. He inflicted his own brand of exquisite torture. The tip of his tongue teased her and tantalised her until she was squirming and moaning for mercy and, eventually, he complied with a low laugh. Had she imagined that note of triumph as she began to pulse around his lips, her body shuddering helplessly as she gripped onto his shoulders? And if she hadn't, what was she going to do about it?

For a while she lay there as she got her breath back, her head buried in his neck, where she couldn't seem to stop fluttering countless kisses against his warm flesh. And once her pulse had stopped its crazy drumming, she pulled away and reached for the bulky ridge of his erection, which was outlined by his denim jeans.

'Louise?' he said unsteadily.

'Your turn, I think,' she said, her voice demure as she carefully eased his zip down over his hardness. 'Lie back.'

She knew he was watching her, as if he were surprised by her cool assertion as she took his rigid shaft into her mouth. She tried to tease him as he had teased her, but it seemed he was too close to the edge to tolerate any such game-playing and the rough sound he made was less a plea and more of a command. She held on to his hips and almost at once she felt him tense, as he shuddered his seed into her waiting mouth.

Eventually she moved to lie beside him and as the silence around them grew, Louise could feel herself being tugged between past and present—like a little boat bobbing around on choppy waters. She badly wanted to make love with him properly. There was nothing she wanted more than to be joined with Giacomo Volterra again, but she was still so scared of doing that, for so many different reasons. Her pulse picked up speed. What a dangerous game she was playing...

After a while he pushed a strand of hair away from her flushed face and stared down at her.

'You're very good at that,' he observed.

She shrugged. 'You were the one who taught me everything I know.'

He traced the shape of her lips with his finger. 'Has there been anyone else?' he asked suddenly.

She saw something very primeval in his eyes as she shook her head. 'Of course not. I made my vows to you, and we're still married.'

'And that's why there's been nobody else?' he demanded. 'Because of the vows you made on your wedding day?'

'There's a reason why I gave my virginity to you,

Giacomo,' she said quietly. 'Nobody had ever made me feel like that before. And that reason hasn't gone away.'

The slow smile he gave indicated his satisfaction with her answer, though on some level she noted she wasn't confident enough to ask him the same question.

'It strikes me as a little ironic,' he murmured, still stroking her hair, 'that we're now in a situation of extended foreplay which never happened the first time around.'

'And does that irritate you?'

'It frustrates me but it doesn't irritate me.' There was silence for a moment. 'Nothing about you irritates me,' he said, at last.

His smoky words were probably nothing other than the lazy commendation offered by a sexually satisfied man, but right now it felt too much like a compliment for comfort. It made her remember all the hopes and dreams she'd woven last time they'd been here. It reminded Louise that she needed to extract herself from his arms before she started building baseless fantasies of the happy-ever-after variety. She closed her eyes, her actions contradicting her intentions, because her limbs felt as heavy as lead. 'Better move.'

'Not yet.' His finger tiptoed a path from neck to instantly peaking nipple as if to demonstrate how instantly he could arouse her. 'I have a proposition to put to you.'

Her dreamy bubble of contentment was dissolved by the sudden gritty note of resolve in his voice. She opened her eyes. 'What?'

'You were only supposed to be here for three days, weren't you?' he said slowly.

'That's what's written in my contract. What of it?'

'I'm just thinking that three days might not be long enough.'

She kept her voice neutral. 'Long enough for what?'

'Parts of my memory have returned, *sì*, but much of it is still missing.' He skated his hand over the naked curve of her hip. 'Meanwhile, you and I seem to have forged a kind of truce, *cara*.'

She didn't like that term. A truce suggested a temporary lull in an ongoing battle.

But wasn't that exactly what divorce was all about?

She wriggled away from the distraction of his fingers. 'Where exactly are you going with this, Giacomo?'

'I need to return to Milan. There are things I can't get out of. And also, that was where we spent some of those lost months, which could act as a prompt for the parts of my memory which still haven't returned.' His eyes burned. 'Which is why I think we should revert to Plan A.'

CHAPTER TEN

THIS TIME LOUISE didn't shun the cashmere coat or the wide-brimmed hat which matched it so perfectly, because they were vital props for her latest reincarnation. As the private jet descended towards the festive lights of Milan, she thought about what she was doing—which by any stretch of the imagination was insane.

She had agreed to return to Italy as Giacomo's wife!

'Plan A,' he had drawled when they'd been lying half naked in front of the roaring fire at Barton, his fingers on her flesh—distracting her and shoring up the feelings of confusion which had been building up inside her ever since she'd stepped over the threshold of his English mansion.

To describe it as Plan A was mildly insulting yet she had allowed him to persuade her to go through with a charade fraught with potential emotional danger. Was that because she had been feeling deliciously sated in his arms, or just unwilling to say goodbye to him yet? Wasn't that closer to the truth? Probably. Louise smoothed her fingers over the fine wool of her designer dress. She needed to remember not to take her new role *too* seriously. Because she wasn't a wife at all. She was a memory aide. And that was what he wanted her for.

To play a part.

To pretend to be something she wasn't.

To facilitate something *he* wanted.

Because Giacomo's reputation was as important to him as his memory and he wanted her as a distraction. He wanted her to draw attention away from the fact that the powerful billionaire might not be firing on all cylinders, by creating a fake marriage to confuse the world who was always watching him. That was what he had announced when he'd turned up at the offices of Posh Catering and nothing had changed since then.

The strange sexual intimacy which had evolved between them didn't count for anything. It was simply the cherry on the cake. She was a means to an end, that was all. And if she allowed a few candid conversations and amazing orgasms to distract her from her primary purpose in his life, she had only herself to blame if that made her unhappy. He hadn't promised her anything, or given her hope. He hadn't started opening up to her, or showing any indication that he would. He certainly hadn't implied that he wanted to commit properly to any relationship, least of all theirs—quite the opposite in fact. He was still a closed book in so many ways.

Yet there was still something unfinished between them.

He still didn't know about the baby.

The sharp pain of recall momentarily took her breath away. Deep down she knew that if Giacomo's memory hadn't wholly returned by the end of her stay, she needed to ask him if it was time for her to fill in all the missing gaps. She would tell him about her miscarriage if he wanted her to, and surely that would give them *both* closure.

She closed her eyes.

It wasn't something she was looking forward to.

'We're coming in to land,' said a soft female voice. 'Welcome to Milan, Signora Volterra. It is good to see you back.'

'Grazie,' said Louise, her lashes fluttering open to see the stewardess whose sparkly diamond ring suggested a recent engagement. Better not disillusion her on the subject of marriage. She forced a big smile. 'It's good to be back.'

Once the stewardess had gone, Giacomo looked up from his laptop, dark eyebrows raised.

'Did you mean that?' he questioned drily.

'I'm just playing my role with aplomb, as requested. Though if you're asking whether I'm enjoying being whisked around in luxury—then the answer would have to be yes. I'd forgotten how easy it was to go anywhere if you had this amount of money at your disposal.' She gave a rueful smile. 'It certainly beats standing in line for hours at the airport.'

'But my wealth didn't tempt you into staying,' he pointed out. 'That might have been a big enough incentive for a lot of women to remain in a bad marriage, but not you.'

'Ah, what price contentment?' she said lightly. 'All the money in the world doesn't count for anything, if you don't have that.'

His eyes narrowed thoughtfully but he made no comment as they descended the aircraft steps to where a limousine was waiting on the tarmac. Louise reminded herself that as far as Giacomo was concerned, it seemed to be business as usual. He had worked throughout the flight, hadn't he? Then announced that they were expected at some party later on this evening and one tomorrow night, too. He was throwing her in at the deep end of Milanese society, without wondering if she might find it all a bit much. Hadn't it occurred to him that her appearance might throw up more questions than it answered?

But she couldn't deny feeling conflicted at being back in his beautiful apartment which overlooked the lush botanical gardens of the city's university. The high-ceilinged rooms and polished wooden floors provided the perfect setting for the contemporary furniture which filled it, and vases of fragrant red roses had been dotted throughout the rooms—presumably to celebrate their arrival. It had always seemed so daunting to her before, but not any more. Although it remained an essentially masculine residence, she was able to appreciate its stylish beauty, rather than find fault with it. Perhaps now she had accepted she had no place here, she was able to view it with dispassionate eyes.

Which wasn't quite so simple where Giacomo was concerned.

She wondered if she was on a road to nowhere, with ideas which now seemed flaky rather than the brainwave she'd originally thought. Her insistence on stopping short of full sex was supposed to provide her with a degree of immunity. So why did her emotions keep getting involved, no matter how hard she tried to fight it? Was it because over Christmas Giacomo had demonstrated a patience and understanding towards her which she hadn't been expecting? Which had dazzled her and charmed her, despite her determination *not* to be either of those things.

His permanent staff were waiting to greet them—a married couple who lived in an apartment on the floor below and who seemed genuinely overjoyed to see her again. Rosa enveloped her in a huge hug and Louise suddenly felt her eyes filling up.

'What's the matter?' asked Giacomo, once they were alone.

'Nothing.'

'You had tears in your eyes.'

She threw him a mocking glance. 'Not your area of expertise, I wouldn't have thought, Giacomo. You once told me you despised the way women turned their tears on and off, and it was easier to ignore them.'

He appeared momentarily chastened by her response and for a while he paced up and down the room, as if he were measuring its dimensions with his long stride. Without warning he came to a sudden halt and began to speak, with the deliberation of someone reading from an autocue.

'I can picture you in a blue dress, by candlelight, and you're supposed to be eating but you're not. You get up and you walk away from the table and you're… you're crying,' he said, his voice growing thick. 'Did I make you cry, Louise?'

She was totally unprepared for the question. Maybe that was why she was able to answer it with total honesty.

'Of course you did,' she said in a low voice. 'Show me a woman who says she never cried when her marriage was breaking down and I'll show you a liar.'

Silently, he evaluated this. 'What did I do that was so awful?'

She thought what a gift this question would have been had he asked it when they'd been living together—a long list of resentments compiled during his many absences would have been presented to him with a flourish. But now that their marriage was over, it merited a different kind of answer. This wasn't about anger or blame or retribution, she reminded herself. It was about healing. For both of them.

'When we arrived back here after that first Christmas, you seemed to want to push me away. We'd been happy in England, or so I thought. And then suddenly, everything changed.' She stared out of the window at the distant spire of a church, just visible above the treetops, and it reminded her of all the times she'd sat there, alone. 'For a start, you were never here.'

His jaw tightened. 'What do you mean, I was never here?'

He was on the defensive, she thought. And for a man who never liked being wrong and rarely admitted to it, this wasn't surprising.

'You travelled so much when we got back to Milan,' she said slowly. 'You were away for so much of the time, I hardly ever saw you. And when I did, there was never time for much more than the basics. We never really talked. We never really got to know one another. With each day that passed, we were growing apart—and we hadn't really known each other that well in the first place.'

He nodded and in the clever contemporary lighting of the high-ceilinged room, his facial scar was barely noticeable. All Louise could see was the gleam of his black eyes and the dramatic darkness of his raven hair and she felt the twist of something she didn't want, or need. He looked like the man she had married and her body was reacting to him in exactly the same way as it had done back then. Not just her body, but her heart, too. She felt a surge of indignation. Was she fated to always want him like this? Not just physically but in every which way. To accept on some level that, for the rest of her life, every other man she met would be a pale imitation of him. If only *her* memory had been wiped clean, wouldn't that have been kinder to them both?

'But you must have known what my life was like when you married me, Louise,' he said, his rich voice breaking into the muddle of her thoughts. 'I am the head of an international company with outlets all over the world. I have never made any secret of my ambition and as long as my business continues to grow, I have commitments.'

'Of course I realised that, but—'

'You thought you could change me, is that it?' He elevated his eyebrows. 'Isn't that the mistake people have been making since the beginning of time, with inevitable consequences?'

She wished he had expressed himself a little differently—or maybe he intended to remind her that she was just one in a long line of women. Women who had come before her—and possibly since—who had tried and failed to make him into the man of their dreams. 'I thought *you* might want to change. Surely everyone has to adapt when they move from single life to being part of a couple?'

'And did you? Were you as adaptable as you wanted me to be?'

She met the challenge in his eyes and tried to answer as honestly as she could. 'I upped sticks and came to Milan, where I didn't know a soul. I started learning the language. I tried my best to fit into your life.'

'But your tone suggests you may have been unsuccessful,' he observed shrewdly. 'Why was that?'

His astute questions were tumbling her defences and Louise felt exposed beneath the cashmere dress, which clung to her body like chocolate sauce poured over an ice-cream cone. Almost instinctively, her fingers crept up to touch the yellow diamond star which dangled above her breasts, and as his gaze followed the movement she could feel her nipples pebbling in response, as if he were able to control her response to him by just the narrowed flash of his dark eyes.

How did he *do* that? she wondered as she forced herself to admit what she had never been able to face up to at the time. Because in some ways it had been easier to walk away from the marriage than to admit her own part in its decline. 'Maybe my insecurity came about because I was so different from all the other women you'd dated before.' She sucked in a deep breath and, as she waited for the remark that didn't come, she gave a wry smile. 'I notice that's something you *don't* deny.'

'How can I when it's true?' His ebony gaze clashed with hers. 'But I didn't marry any of the others, did I?'

'No.'

His voice was rough. 'And you know why not? You know what was different about you?'

She froze and felt the trickle of ice snaking its way down her spine. Had he remembered the pitifully short life of their unborn child, which had brought the curtain down on their ill-starred union?

'Tell me, Giacomo,' she whispered. 'Tell me why you married me.'

'Because of this,' he husked savagely as he walked across the room and pulled her into his arms. *'This.'*

His touch was electric but his answer was brutal. It shouldn't have shocked her but it did—yet deep down it was exactly as she had suspected. It had just been an incredible physical chemistry between two

very different people, which had resulted in repercussions neither of them had been expecting. And
despite the temptation of his seeking kiss and the
answering heat of her own body, for once Louise
didn't capitulate.

'No,' she said fervently, pulling away from him
and hoping he wouldn't notice that she was trembling. She walked over to the window and stared
down at the Christmas lights sparkling over Milan,
before turning back to him again. 'I don't need any
reward therapy, Giacomo.'

He regarded her blankly. 'Reward therapy?'

'Isn't sex a variation on buying a woman jewels,
or taking her on a fancy holiday? Just something to
keep her quiet.'

Surprisingly, he had started laughing. 'If keeping
a woman quiet is what sex is all about, then it seems
to have failed spectacularly in your case.'

She wanted to tell him not to laugh like that because she couldn't cope with his own seductive brand
of humour. She wanted him to display all his flaws
so she could concentrate on those and remind herself why she was better off without him. She kept
her voice low. 'We can't go on like this, Giacomo,'
she said. 'Couples who are on the brink of divorce
don't behave like this. We're not teenagers and it's
messing with my head. So why don't we do what we
should have done in the first place?'

'Which is, what?' he drawled.

'We keep a sensible physical distance between us for the next few days and hope your memory returns in the meantime.'

There was silence for a long moment. 'And if it doesn't?' he said, at last.

She hesitated, uncomfortable beneath that flinty gaze but determined to brazen it out, despite her body's screaming objection. Because this was for the best. Not just for her, but for both of them. 'Then I'll answer any questions you might have and tell you anything you want to know. Anything at all.' She smoothed her dress down, more for something to do with her hands than for any other reason. 'How does that sound?'

'Honestly?' His mouth grew hard. 'It sounds like hell.'

Giacomo watched Louise from the other side of the room. She meant it. She had meant every damned word of the fervent little declaration she'd made last night and which she had then demonstrated by taking herself off to sleep separately, with not even a goodnight kiss to remember her by. The sexual perks of this strange reunion were over. From now on he could look but he most definitely could not touch.

He looked.

And, *Madonna mia*, she was worth looking at. A

ragged sigh left his lungs. The most beautiful woman he had ever seen. Had he ever told her that, he wondered, or had his tight-lipped arrogance simply left her to assume that he found her immensely pleasing to the eye?

Like many of the other women at the party, she wore a black dress—but Louise's take on a simple garment elevated it to an entirely different level. Her abundant curves ensured that she projected a warmth and sexuality which nobody else in the room possessed and which seemed to draw every other man's eyes to her, as if she were a magnet. She stood by a window which overlooked Milan's famous cathedral, beside which a giant fir tree sparkled. Behind her, giant flakes of snow were swirling in a golden swarm against the flamboyance of the seasonal lights. His car had dropped them off a short while ago and they had walked among the festive throng, making their way along the crowded streets to the sound of festive music echoing through the Piazza del Duomo. Once again, he had been filled with an unfamiliar lightness of spirit, which had made him feel curiously relaxed.

And now they were here at Alessio Cavalcante's famous post-Christmas party—an invitation to which was highly sought after in the rarefied circles of the city in which Giacomo mixed. Usually, he had a lot of time for Alessio—the two men had grown up in similar, deprived circumstances and had much in common. So why was he currently feeling as if he'd like to pick up one of his oldest friends by the scruff of his neck and hurl him out onto the snow? Would it have anything to do with the fact that Alessio had been monopolising his wife since they'd arrived and all he could feel was the slow, black burn of jealousy?

She was *his* wife.

Except that she wasn't.

He shook his head as a waitress offered him an arancino, unable to escape the torture of his thoughts. He must have been a bad person for her to have walked away, because he sensed that a woman like Louise wouldn't give up on a marriage unless she really had to. Hadn't he seen concern, even tenderness on her face sometimes, when she'd thought he wasn't looking? When she had slowly touched the scars on his back, she had projected a fierce protectiveness which had taken his breath away. Wasn't that one of the reasons why he'd never mentioned the other stuff? The bitter stuff he couldn't bear to remember. The hungry days and long, cold nights. The way people looked at boys like him who had nothing, or no one. Wasn't he afraid that her innate softness might swamp him and leave him feeling raw and vulnerable, if he confided in her? He had worn his heavy emotional armour for so long that he couldn't imagine ever removing it.

He saw her laugh at something Alessio had said,

her hair swinging around her shoulders like a glossy curtain. He watched her chink glasses and nod rather intently before taking a sip of champagne and, again, he felt that dark coil of fury deep inside him.

'Giacomo?'

He turned to see a woman who had suddenly appeared by his side and was slanting her long-lashed eyes at him. She was stick-thin, her skirt was outrageously short and her waist-length hair the colour of ripe corn. She was a very famous model he'd met on a handful of occasions in the past and he knew that she had tried to contact him when he'd lain in that Swiss clinic, because his aide had told him. Many men considered her beautiful, but Giacomo had ignored all her overtures and ordered that the exquisite arrangement of white flowers she had sent to his bedside should be dispatched home immediately with his favourite nurse.

'*Ciao*, Daniela,' he replied.

'You're looking good. Very good.' The look in her eyes was unashamedly appreciative. 'You've recovered, I see?'

'I have.'

'Nice to see you back.' She followed the direction of his gaze, which had inevitably returned to drink in the delicious sight of Louise's abundant flesh. 'Though I'm guessing her presence here means you're off the market?'

'Her name is Louise,' he answered coolly. 'And I hate to disappoint you, but I was never on the market. I am not a piece of fish.' He crinkled her a smile to soften the blow. 'And now, if you will excuse me.'

He saw the disappointment which crumpled her red lips and, compelled by an instinct he had no desire to control, he walked across the room towards Louise, who was still deep in conversation with his friend.

'Ah, Giacomo.' Alessio's voice was smooth as they both looked up. 'Such a delight to see Louise again. Though I notice she's refusing to be pinned down about an invitation extended to you both to come to my Umbrian house for Easter. In fact, I'm getting the distinct feeling she isn't planning to stay that long. Isn't there anything you can do to persuade her otherwise?'

Giacomo felt a mixture of outrage and indignation. Wasn't she supposed to be playing the part of his wife? How dared she hint at her plans with someone else, especially when she had not discussed the exact date of her departure with *him*?

'We will be sure to keep you posted,' he said blandly, snaking an arm around his wife's waist in an overtly possessive gesture. 'Thanks for a wonderful evening, Alessio. Louise, are you ready to leave?'

He saw the look of surprise in her eyes and the faint flicker of resentment which followed it but she did well not to challenge him, because the way he was feeling right then, he might very well have thrown her over his shoulder and carried her out of the glittering party.

And just imagine what *that* would have done to his super-cool reputation, he thought grimly.

She didn't say a word as someone fetched her coat, was tight-lipped as they recrossed the Piazza del Duomo, and it wasn't until they were in the car and it was purring back towards his apartment that she turned on him with anger spitting from her eyes.

'Just what is your *problem*?' she demanded.

'My problem? You think I enjoy the sight of my wife flirting with another man?'

'Oh, for goodness' sake—I was *talking* to him. That's what people are supposed to do at parties. They laugh. They joke. They raise their glasses and wish each other Happy Christmas—'

'Buon Natale,' he corrected automatically.

'They don't stand in one corner of the room with a face like thunder, acting like a reborn Neanderthal,' she raged on, as if he hadn't spoken. 'I don't understand, Giacomo. You never *used* to be jealous. The very opposite, in fact. We hardly ever used to go out and when we did, you used to be so tightly controlled.'

And with those words she unleashed something inside him. It was a moment of unwanted epiphany.

Like the untethering of a helium balloon which then floated up into the sky. Giacomo's mouth was dry as he stared out of the car window, his pulse pounding as the bright blur of the city lights passed them by.

His memory hadn't magically been returned to him wholesale—other than the sporadic episodes he'd been experiencing for a while now. But suddenly he recognised that his determination to keep all the other stuff buried away—the bitter, unsavoury stuff—might be acting as some kind of barrier.

But it was more than just wanting his memories back.

He wanted Louise.

He wanted her very badly. Not just in his bed but in his life. Not just now, but for ever.

How had it taken so long for him to realise that?

Had it only just occurred to him that the Christmas they'd just spent in England had been happy—as it had been once before, soon after they were married? And then they had come back to Milan and it had all gone wrong.

Why was that?

He turned to look at her but she was staring fixedly at the fingers which were clasped in her lap as if she couldn't bear to meet his eyes. And he wondered then if he could bear to reveal his soul to her. His dark and empty soul.

As far as he could see, he had no choice.

CHAPTER ELEVEN

LOUISE'S SIMMERING MOOD was still in evidence when Giacomo closed the door of the apartment behind them and worked out what he was going to say to her. He watched as she removed her coat, the light bouncing off her glossy hair, and he was suddenly filled with an overwhelming desire to run his fingers through it.

'I'm off to bed now,' she said, reaching for the sparkly little bag she'd placed on the hall table.

'No.'

'No?' She jerked back, a look of surprise on her face. 'How very authoritarian of you, Giacomo! Haven't you forgotten I'm supposed to be your wife now, not your obedient housekeeper? And since there's nobody around to see us, we can stop all the play-acting. And I'm very tired. I found that party quite draining. So if it's all right with you, I'll say goodnight. We can talk in the morning.'

'Please?' he said, and he saw her hesitate—a flicker of uncertainty replacing the feisty defiance.

'Have you learnt how powerful that little word can be when you hardly ever say it?' she questioned huskily, her voice a little unsteady. 'Is that your favourite manipulative tool?'

'Or maybe it's a genuine question?' he parried softly. 'All I'm asking is that you come and sit by the fire with me for a while, because I want to talk to you.'

Her body stiffening, she met his gaze. 'You've remembered something?'

'No.' He shook his head. 'This is something I've known all along. Something I've never forgotten, no matter how much I've wished I could.'

He saw something alter in her expression, as if she'd recognised that the rules of the game had suddenly changed.

'Okay,' she said cautiously.

She led the way into the sitting room and sat down on one of the sofas and he thought how at ease she seemed here, despite the sudden watchfulness which had darkened her extraordinary blue eyes. Rosa must have lit the fire and put a silver tray of drinks on a table, next to an elaborate display of roses and berries, which scented the air. It occurred to him that for once the elegant room seemed almost...*homely*.

Was that because she was there? 'Drink?' he said, gesturing towards a decanter of brandy.

She looked up as she crossed one elegant leg over the other—a movement he found momentarily distracting. 'Why, do you think I'll need one?'

He shook his head and walked over to stand close to the fire in an attempt to warm his skin, which suddenly felt ice-cold. He thought how best to frame his words until he realised this wasn't like those presentations he'd given in his early years, when he'd been eager to acquire the confidence and funding of his potential backers. He wasn't standing before the woman he had married seeking judgement or even approval, but to offer an explanation of what had made him the man he was.

In the hope of what?

That she would love him?

Ruthlessly, he crushed the thought. Why give headspace to something he'd never really believed in?

'You were always curious about my childhood,' he began slowly. 'And you must have quickly learnt that I don't like talking about it.'

'You could say that.' She looked flustered, as if she couldn't quite believe that he had voluntarily brought up the subject. As if she couldn't quite believe he might be about to answer all the questions he'd always thrown back at her before.

'So, go ahead,' he continued. 'Ask.'

She uncrossed her legs and pressed her knees very close together. 'Well, I know about your time at the orphanage, because sometimes you referred to that. But you didn't go there until you were eleven, did you?'

'No,' he said flatly.

'So...well, it couldn't have been the only defining factor in your life.' She shrugged. 'There must have been a lot which happened before that.'

There was a long pause. 'You're referring to my mother, I assume?'

'The mother you also never talk about,' she affirmed, in a low voice. 'But at least you had a mother. You're lucky.'

'Has it ever occurred to you *why* I don't talk about her?'

'I don't know.' She went very still. 'Because it upsets you too much?'

He gave a laugh which didn't really feel much like a laugh. 'Oh, Louise. How sweetly naïve you can be at times.'

'Maybe because I don't remember either of my parents!' she retorted, with a return of customary fire. 'That could be one of the reasons why I sentimentalise parenthood, don't you think?'

'Or maybe you're the lucky one,' he said slowly. His words tailed away but she didn't prompt him.

Maybe if she had he would have clammed up—as deep down he really wanted to. But he was aware that time was running out for them and something was telling him he needed to resurrect the past if he was going to stand any chance of leaving it behind. To drag it up from that dark place where he'd buried it so long ago.

'She was a single mother,' he began. 'But she never let that cramp her lifestyle, which was…how best to describe it? Energetic,' he concluded with a grim twist of his mouth. 'We lived in a tenement block in Turin and whenever she wanted to go out, she left me with whichever neighbour happened to be around. Or not. I was on my own a lot and learned how to fend for myself. To find food from somewhere. Anywhere. I guess you could have described me as feral.'

'That must have been…hard.'

He shrugged. 'You accept what you get given. It was all I knew. I became known as the kid whose mother didn't want a kid. That I could deal with. The worst thing was when she used to bring her boyfriends back to the room.' His mouth hardened. 'That wasn't much fun. She used to tell me that things would get better, but they never did. Just like she used to tell me she would be home at a certain time, but she never was. I learnt I could never trust a word she said.'

She flinched. 'And your father? Wasn't he ever around?'

'No.' He waited for a moment before he answered her and, again, his instinct was not to elaborate, to bite it back as he'd always done before. But something about the expression in her eyes made it hard for him to look away and Giacomo found himself being drawn into that soft and compelling gaze. 'I only met him once. Much later. He wasn't a local.' A ragged breath left his lungs. 'He was visiting Turin from Naples when they hooked up for one night.'

'Like us, you mean?' she questioned, her voice suddenly growing wooden.

'No. Nothing like us. Because I saw you a *lot* in those early days, didn't I?' he questioned suddenly, his mind clearing a little.

'Yes. Yes, you did.' She nodded. 'Carry on with your story. If…if you want to.'

Giacomo wondered how best to summarise the bleak discovery of his father's attitude towards him before grimly accepting there was no way to make it palatable. He'd never talked about this, he realised. Not to a living soul. Not just because of the shame, but because there was a limit to another person's insight. Because nobody really understood what it felt like to be hungry unless they'd been hungry themselves. Just as nobody could ever imagine how bad it felt to have those low-life wasters his mother had associated with look at you as if you were something the cat dragged in. Or a father who regarded you with nothing but cold contempt in his eyes. He'd kept it to himself because he didn't want to be judged, but something told him that Louise would never judge him.

'I guess things would have gone on in that way until I was old enough to make my own way in the world. Living close to the edge, but just about sur-viving—until my mother became ill.'

'Oh, Giacomo,' she whispered, as if the tone in his voice had warned her about what he was about to say.

'Save your sympathy.' With an abrupt slicing movement of his hand, he cut her short. 'She brought it on herself. It was a case of one botched plastic sur-gery too many, in a seedy, downtown clinic. She de-veloped sepsis and with only hours to live, she told me about my father for the first time. She said he was one of the wealthiest men in the country.' He ran his tongue over suddenly dry lips, remembering the choked words which she'd uttered, in between those terrible gasps for air. Of a man with an impossible wealth. 'She said she'd tried to contact him before with no success, and although she hadn't been sur-prised, things were different now. That in the circum-stances he would take me in and see me right. He would protect his son, because all men wanted sons.'

'And…did he?'

Giacomo swallowed. It still hurt to think about it, that was the extraordinary thing. Even after all these years.

He looked into Louise's blue eyes but he didn't really see them. He was back in the past, on that early morning a quarter of a century ago, when the sun was already unbearably hot in the sky. 'I went to see him the day after my mother's funeral, slipping aboard the first train bound for Naples, terrified the authorities would find me and send me to the orphanage.' The pictures in his head were vivid and coming fast on top of each other. Scruffy and unkempt, he had used his wits and cunning to find and gain access to a vast villa outside the city, right on the Peninsula Sorrentina. With its vineyard and sea views, its marble floors and chandeliers, it had been a place of such unbelievable splendour that Giacomo had felt as if he had walked into paradise.

Had he really believed that its billionaire owner would scoop him up and take him under his wing?

Maybe he had. Because hadn't there been one remaining flicker of hope in a heart which had felt battered and drained? But after he'd blurted out his story, the man's face had been as cold as marble and Giacomo had fished out a faded photo when asked his mother's name.

'It's Loredana, sir,' he had stuttered out. 'Here… here she is.'

The tycoon had stared at it with unhidden contempt for a long minute before shaking his head.

'He claimed never to have seen my mother in his life, but he called out for someone called Roberto, and that's when a man strolled into the room and I froze as I saw the two men standing side by side. The billionaire and his bodyguard. My father was the bodyguard. I recognised him instantly, we were so alike. Apparently, he often used to pretend to be his wealthy boss because it used to guarantee him a one hundred per cent success rate whenever he wanted to get a woman into bed.'

There was silence for a moment while she absorbed this. 'And how did he react when you told him?' she questioned, at last. 'I'm assuming you told him?'

'Sì, I told him.' Giacomo's mouth felt as if someone had poured concrete into it, for he could barely get the words out. 'He said he'd never wanted to be a father and if he did, he certainly wouldn't choose some kid from the slums with a whore for a mother.'

He saw her face contort and he wanted to lash out and tell her he didn't want her damned pity. But she was already on her feet, walking over to where he stood, and she was wrapping her arms around his neck and he could feel her—all that sweet, soft weight of her—pressing against him.

'Giacomo,' she said, in between whispering kisses all over his face.

And he let her.

Actually, that was a lie. He was kissing her back as if his life depended on it, and maybe it did. He wanted to tell her to give him time to catch his breath, because he could feel control leeching from his body and if he stalled it would give him time to compose himself. It would put him back in the driving seat, which was where he most liked to be. Or was he just kidding himself, when there was only one place he wanted to be right now and that was in her arms?

'Giacomo,' Louise said again, and emotion flooded through her as she opened her lips to his and kissed him as deeply as she knew how. There was so much he'd told her. Stuff which made her understand him more, but way too much to process now. There was only one thing they needed to do now. Because didn't instinct tell her that her estranged husband needed her right now, as he had never needed her before?

She thought she was his equal?

So start acting like one.

She pulled away from him. 'Let's go to bed,' she whispered.

Without another word, he took her hand and silently they moved through the darkened apartment, from the rose-scented room to the bedroom which once she had shared with him. She didn't focus on the peculiarity of being back in a place which held so much emotional significance for her—or a bed where she had known great pleasure but also much distress—she just slid the buttons from his shirt with unsteady fingers, while he dealt with the zip of her dress.

It wasn't an occasion for admiring lingerie or feasting their eyes over slowly revealed flesh. This was urgent. Hungry. Efficiently, they stripped off each other's clothes until they were both naked and wrapped tightly in each other's arms and lying on the bed, skin against skin, and it could have felt unbearably poignant, except that it didn't. Louise closed her eyes.

It felt right.

So right.

Their lips met and their bodies melded. Time blurred as they stroked and kissed. He was pressed against her and the weight of his arousal felt heavy as she felt it nudging close to where she was slick and ready. Everything seemed to be happening in slow motion yet it also seemed to be happening very fast.

She said only one thing.

'Protection?'

He gave a muffled curse as he fished around in the bedside table until he had found what he had been looking for, and as he slid it carefully over his erec-tion Louise told herself she wasn't going to allow herself to think about the consequences of what she was about to do—all she wanted was to feel him deep inside her.

She gave a sharp intake of breath as he entered her and for a moment he stilled.

'Okay?' he questioned, looking down into her face.

'Mmm.' She bit her lip as he began to move. 'It's—'

'I know it is,' he said, in an odd kind of voice. 'I know.'

For a while it was nothing but rhythm and sen-sation. Each kiss growing deeper. Each long stroke sending her higher and then higher still. He filled her completely, just as he'd always done. He felt part of her, just as he'd always done. She was aware that they had done this many times before. But this time it felt different. It *was* different. He might not be her husband for very much longer, but while he was—couldn't she love him? If not with words, then surely with her body?

Her fingers caressed him, her lips drifting over every available inch of skin. She could feel the beckon of her orgasm and she tried to delay it because she didn't want this ever to end. But she couldn't. Of course she couldn't. Giacomo was way too good a lover for that. Within seconds she was shuddering out her pleasure and she could feel the exquisite tension in his body just before he followed her.

'Lulu,' he groaned.

And that was her complete undoing. The moment when she shattered so completely that she wasn't sure she could ever be made whole again.

She was Lulu again.

His Lulu.

For a while she didn't speak, she was filled with a hope which she couldn't seem to suppress. It glimmered like a flame inside her, growing brighter by the second. She lay there holding him very tightly until the frantic sound of their ragged breathing had grown steady. If only she were able to keep that moment and bottle it—this moment of perfect harmony. He had opened up to her for the first time ever and then they'd made love. Properly. Couldn't those things be the bedrock on which they might be able to rebuild their relationship?

She turned her head to look at him, but he was staring up at the ceiling and he didn't move or try to catch her eye, even though he must have known she wanted him to. She thought his profile looked *unfamiliar* and that his body had suddenly grown tense. A sudden arrow of fear shafted through her.

Had she really been lying there thinking they might be able to start again? Had she forgotten what he'd said to her? The one thing which could never be unsaid. Or forgotten.

'Giacomo?' she said.

He turned then and it seemed she hadn't imagined the tension at all. His eyes were like stone and a deep foreboding made her body stiffen as she waited for what suddenly felt inevitable.

His words were edged with a quality she didn't recognise.

'There was a baby, wasn't there?'

CHAPTER TWELVE

TIME STOOD STILL in that Milanese bedroom and it was as silent as the grave.

'Yes,' Louise said, at last. 'There was a baby. A baby I miscarried at fourteen weeks.'

Giacomo said nothing, just peeled himself away from her and got out of bed, disappearing into the en suite bathroom before returning, wearing a silk robe. And now she felt a tremor of apprehension because he never wore a robe, unless one of the staff was around.

'Why didn't you tell me this before?'

She tried to compose herself and not to crumble beneath what sounded like condemnation in his voice. 'Because you specifically told me you didn't want an information dump. You said you wanted to remember organically.'

He snapped on one of the lamps so that light flooded over them and she wished he hadn't because now it felt as if she were in an interrogation chamber.

'And that's the only reason?'

Louise opened her mouth to say yes, until she realised there were two ways she could proceed with this. She could bluster and tell him that since he had kept *his* secrets, why shouldn't she keep hers? But they weren't playing a game of tit-for-tat. Hadn't she vowed from the beginning to be honest with him?

And hadn't he vowed to do the same?

Their marriage was clearly at its end stage—what point was there in keeping stuff from him now? Shouldn't she confess all the things he didn't know, even if he didn't like what he heard? Even if it hurt to say them. 'No, not the only reason. I was scared.' But the lump in her throat was so big, she couldn't get her next words out.

His eyes narrowed. 'Scared of what?'

'The pain of talking about it, mostly,' she admitted, telling herself she must not break down and cry. 'I didn't want to revisit it. I didn't want to have that conversation—and I thought my actions were justified. You certainly didn't want to discuss it at the time—so why would you want to now? We were already going through some difficult times in our marriage, and when it happened you were away in America. Chicago, I think it was. There it is again— that ever-persistent inconsequential detail again!' She wiped the back of her hand over her eyes and sniffed. 'I couldn't get hold of you and by the time

I did, it was… Well, it was all over. And when you came back to Italy, I realised…'

'What did you realise?' he questioned quietly as her words faded away for a second time.

Realising that she was going to have to leave that room some time soon and it was best to make her escape by stages, Louise sat up and pulled up the duvet to cover her nakedness. But the stupid thing was that she still felt exposed beneath the glare of his burning black gaze. An unbearable sense of sadness washed over her and now it was harder to keep the tears at bay. 'I realised that the marriage was over, too,' she said thickly. 'Maybe that shouldn't have come as a shock, because we were already living on borrowed time. I was pregnant when you married me.'

'I know.'

'You've remembered that?'

'I've remembered everything,' he said.

She rubbed the edge of the duvet between her thumb and forefinger, staring at it intently before lifting her eyes to him again. 'You probably wouldn't have married me if I hadn't been carrying your baby, but you were adamant that you wanted to—which surprised me. But now you've told me about your mother, I think I can understand why. I suspect it was your own sense of responsibility which made you do it—because you didn't want to be accused of deserting your own child, as your father had done to you. Which was very, well...*decent* of you,' she added carefully.

'Decent?' he echoed, in a strangled kind of voice.

Louise knew she'd probably said enough and there was no reason to say any more, but something was spurring her on. Because in a funny kind of way she needed this. It felt like some strange kind of exorcism, which would hopefully rid her of the ghosts from the past and let her walk into the future unencumbered and free. She might come down with an almighty crash tomorrow, but—as Scarlett O'Hara had once said—tomorrow was another day.

'There's nothing wrong with decency,' she said quickly. 'It's a very underrated attribute. You never said things you didn't mean, Giacomo. You never told me you loved me. It was nothing but a practical marriage.' She hesitated, because this was probably the hardest thing of all. 'Do you remember what you said when you came back to Italy afterwards?'

'I told you,' he said flatly. 'I remember everything.'

His face had grown so tense that Louise wondered if it had been a below-the-belt remark to remind him of this—especially now. But didn't confession traditionally offer absolution? And maybe Giacomo needed some of that as badly as she did.

'Tell me,' she breathed, wondering if it was going to hurt as much this time around. 'Tell me what you remember.'

'It was when you were wearing that blue dress. It was the first time I'd seen you since it had happened. I remember it felt awkward. I didn't have the right words. Maybe there weren't any. I said...' He paused for a moment, before continuing. 'I said that it was probably all for the best. The miscarriage,' he added, as if she needed that brutal clarification. 'And that's when you started crying.'

'Can you blame me?' she whispered. 'When you said that, there wasn't really any way back from there, Giacomo. Surely you can see that.'

'I can see that now,' he breathed, and now his voice seemed to crack, like a glass plunged into boiling water. 'All I can say is how...how sorry I am.'

'You were only being honest,' she said. His apology had been something she'd always craved but now she realised that she was actually defending him. Had time and distance given her clarity? 'You never planned for a baby. You never planned to get married either. And afterwards, I knew there was no reason to stay—to pin you down with something you didn't want. I couldn't face having that discussion and having to face yet more guilt and anguish and that's why I left without telling you.'

'Sì.'

He seemed to absorb this, his face like dark stone, before his jaw briefly tightened—as if he had just come to some sort of resolution. He stood as motionless as a statue, a composition of shadow and muscle, with all the glittering lights of the city behind him. He had never looked more formidable, nor more untouchable. 'I can't blame you for that, Lu.' He turned to look out at the lights, before grinding out his next statement. 'Why would you want to stay with a man who could offer you no comfort? Who could only deepen your wounds with his unthinking words?'

Louise shook her head. She didn't want him to suffer like this. Hadn't they both suffered enough already? 'Giacomo?'

Silently, he turned to look at her and more than anything she wanted to remove that terrible look of desolation from his eyes.

'What?'

'Where do we…where do we go from here?'

'Don't worry, Lu.' He gave a thin smile. 'Your tenure as my quasi-wife can now officially be described as having come to an end.'

She blinked. 'So…?'

The smile had vanished and in its place came a look of steely determination. 'I think, taking everything into account, it would be best if you leave as soon as possible. Tomorrow.'

His words made all the breath escape from her lungs. 'You…you want me to leave tomorrow?'

'Of course.' His voice was bland. 'There is no reason for you to remain here, is there? And I have no desire to detain you any longer than is necessary. I have filled in the missing year and am now in possession of all the facts and for that, I must thank you.'

'*Thank* me?' she repeated woodenly.

He nodded. 'I cannot tell you what a relief it is for me to be able to remember.' There was a flicker of something in his black eyes. Something which was gone almost as soon as it had appeared. 'I will arrange for a limo and my plane to be at your disposal. Once the Christmas period is over, I will ensure that our divorce is processed as quickly as possible—you have my word on that. And in the meantime, I think I'd better leave you in peace so that you can get some sleep.' He gave the ghost of a smile, which somehow emphasised the fatigue which had suddenly harshened his features into a weary mask. 'We seem to make a habit of getting ourselves into this complicated bedroom pattern, don't we, Louise?'

Louise couldn't quite believe what he was saying, or why that flat note of resolution suddenly sounded like the most depressing sound she'd ever heard. What she wouldn't have given to have witnessed his fire or his fury. If he'd snapped at her or raged at her for not telling him about their baby sooner, she could have coped with it. Welcomed it, even. If he'd broken down and mourned that lost little life, they could have offered one another comfort. But Giacomo had been badly damaged, she saw that now. Which was why he never let that steely armour slip.

She watched him walking across the bedroom towards the door and wished she could have one last chance. What if she called out to him to ask him, please, to reconsider? Wondered aloud if they couldn't have another stab at their marriage? But she had been determined to maintain her dignity from the get-go, and she didn't want his final memory of her to be one of her *begging* him to try again.

Even so, she wasn't a good enough actress to pin an understanding smile to her lips. She just lay back so he couldn't see her, but he didn't look back in any case. And when the door had shut behind him, she turned and buried her face in the pillow, her shoulders shaking with soft and helpless tears.

She didn't know how long she lay there, crying her heart out until she had no tears left to cry. She tried to imagine her life going forward and, just like before, she was back to running up against a brick wall. She knew Giacomo would be more than fair when it came to their divorce. He would probably settle a generous amount of money on her—possibly even enough for her to start a little business of her own, if she wanted to. That had always been her plan before she'd met him, though at the time it had seemed an impossible dream.

So why did the thought now fill her with dread?

She could do it—of that she had no doubt. She could do anything she wanted if she put her mind to it. Who was to say, with a lot of hard work and imagination, she wouldn't become one of those success stories—the kind which would have inspired someone like her when she was sixteen and just leaving school?

But this vision of the future presented no allure.

She turned onto her back.

Something wasn't right. Despite everything that had happened, it still felt unfinished.

She thought about Giacomo's reaction to what he had learned. How calm he had been.

Too calm.

She thought about the painful flicker in his black eyes which had contradicted the cool indifference on his scarred face.

And then she forced herself to look at her own part in what had just taken place and it wasn't pretty.

He had told her stuff tonight about his childhood which he would never have admitted before and she understood for the first time why pushing her away had always been his default mechanism. He'd never told her he loved her because nobody had ever told him. Or shown him.

Not even her. Even though she had loved him very much. She had been so busy protecting her own feelings—so determined not to get hurt—that she hadn't had the courage of her own convictions.

A wave of resolve washed through her and she knew she had to tell him. It might be too late, but he needed to know. Because relationships weren't a ledger, with balances and checks and careful accounting. You didn't wait to say something until someone said it to *you* first.

Without bothering to contemplate the wisdom of her actions, she jumped out of bed and pulled on a robe—which Rosa had unpacked—and then set out in search of Giacomo. But he wasn't in any of the four bedrooms.

She could feel the mad skitter of her pulse as she moved silently along the darkened corridors of the large apartment. What if he'd let himself out and taken himself off to a hotel, or a friend's, to spend the night—so he wouldn't have to face seeing her again?

She found him in his home office, with its four international clocks lined up on one of the walls, the seconds ticking away and with them, their lives. He was sitting staring at a screen filled with figures but his shoulders were hunched and she wondered if he was actually seeing anything.

'Giacomo?' she said quietly.

He turned round then, and Louise was shocked by the bleakness in his black eyes, but he quickly composed himself.

'Can't sleep?'

'No. I have something I need to tell you,' she said in a low voice.

His face darkened. 'I think we've talked enough for one night, don't you?'

But she carried on as if he hadn't spoken. 'I've been doing a lot of thinking about the past and… well, I think it's important to acknowledge that we were happy for a lot of the time when we were together. There was a thunderbolt, yes—but there was substance, too, because those first few months were amazing. And I've sort of allowed what happened subsequently to make me forget about that time. It culminated in that amazing Christmas we spent at Barton soon after we were married, which was magical.' She sucked in a deep breath. 'But when we got back here to Milan, you were different. Distant.'

'So you said before,' he offered coolly. 'Don't worry about it. I agree that it was my fault.'

'I'm not apportioning blame, Giacomo,' she said quietly. 'I'm just trying to get my head around what happened. I think you cared for me more deeply than you intended—but you had no template for love, or relationships, or fatherhood. You'd been hurt so badly as a child that I don't think you could contemplate ever feeling that kind of pain again. It was easier to reject me, than risk being rejected yourself. That's why you pushed me away and kept on pushing. But

I just took it. I just rolled over and took it, when I should have fought harder. Should have made you talk to me. I should have told you how much I loved you, which I did.' Her voice became a little choked, because this was the hardest part of all, and the biggest gamble of her life. Dignity be damned, she thought irreverently. Didn't Giacomo Volterra, who had been hurt so much, deserve a demonstration of her unconditional love for him? 'Do,' she amended quietly. 'I do love you. Still. Very much.'

'How can you possibly love a man who has been so cruel to you?' he demanded, but his voice was breaking.

'If it was cruelty, it was unwitting,' she said softly.

Giacomo's throat was so tight he could barely breathe because the emotions bubbling up inside him were threatening to overpower him and, more out of habit than desire, he tried to hold them back. But this time they would not be stemmed. He looked at Lu's face, pale as the ghostly light from his computer screen, and saw all the love and understanding that any man could ask for.

Could he? After everything that had happened.

He rose to his feet and saw the way she searched his face. Saw the way she bit her lip as if she hoped— yet didn't dare to hope. Was that because she had noticed the tears which were blurring the vision of a man who had never cried? And suddenly this felt like the hardest thing in the world to say, yet somehow the easiest. He had never said it before because he never said anything he didn't mean. But he meant it now.

'I love you, Lu,' he growled. 'But how can I possibly accept your love after everything I've done?'

'You accept it because I'm giving it to you,' she answered simply. 'It doesn't come with any conditions. If you still want me to go back to England in the morning, then I'll go. I don't want to go, but I will. I don't want to spend the rest of my life without you—but if that's the way it has to be, then I will deal with it. Over to you, Giacomo. The ball, as they say, is in your court.'

He shook his head, unable to hide the admiration he felt for her. 'You are making this impossible for me!'

'Am I? That's good. So what are you going to do about it?'

But that was when the game-playing stopped and he caught hold of her and held her tightly—so tightly. He would never again let her go, he vowed fiercely. He carried her back to their room and once he had settled her in bed, fetched them a drink of water and climbed in beside her, he voiced something else which had been on his mind.

'You weren't just scared of revisiting the pain of the past, were you?' he questioned softly. 'There was another reason why you wouldn't have full sex with me. You said you didn't want us to become too intimate, but there was something else.' There was a pause. 'You were scared of getting pregnant again, weren't you, Lu?'

Louise looked up into his face, thinking what a difference a day made. Before she might have refused to answer a question as direct as this, mostly as a way of protecting her feelings, or maybe not daring to own them. But she didn't have to do that any more and neither did she want to. She wanted them to be able to communicate on every level, no matter if sometimes that made her feel uncomfortable.

'Yes,' she admitted quietly. 'I don't...didn't.' She looked up into his face. 'I don't know what you feel about having children but there's a bit of me which is terrified of taking the risk, in case I miscarry again. And I'm not sure I could go through with it a second time. If that's a deal-breaker for you, I will understand.'

'There is no such thing as a risk-free life,' he whispered, his mouth against her hair. 'We would have the best medical care at our disposal and this time I would be by your side all the time. But you know something? We don't have to have a baby if you don't want to go through the worry of a pregnancy again. Whatever works is fine with me because I love you. Do you understand that? I love you and I want to stay married to you, Lu. Just like you said to me, it doesn't come with any conditions.' He frowned. 'Have I said something wrong? I don't understand. Why are you crying?'

But she was crying and laughing all at the same time and Louise shook her head. 'This time I'm crying because I'm happy,' she whispered, touching her fingertips to his scarred and beautiful face. 'And because I'm lying in the arms of the man I love.'

'Lu...' he said, but his voice was distinctly unsteady as he bent his head and kissed her.

EPILOGUE

CHRISTMAS.

The most wonderful time of the year.

Yes. She would concur with that.

Louise looked out of the mullioned window of the ancient house, her heart brimming over with love and gratitude as she drank in the scene which lay before her. Outside, against the wintry sweep of Barton's expansive grounds, her beloved husband was holding the mittened fingers of their little son, Leonardo, as they walked round and round the giant snowman, admiring their handiwork. And this definitely *was* the most magnificent snowman in the history of the world.

The house was filled with the scent of baking panettone, the giant tree was glittering in the dining room and alongside it stood the carved nativity set—which Louise carefully got out now, year after year. In a while the family would go down to Westover village, to gather in the little square and listen to all the carol singers. Louise made a mental note to herself. She must be sure to pack a pocketful of tissues for when Leo joined in with 'Away in a Manger', in his adorable little voice, because that reedy rendition got to her—every time.

She gave a contented sigh as she contemplated going to wake their other son—the mischievous toddler, Dante, who would wreak merry havoc from the moment he opened his eyes. She was so happy. Happier than she'd ever believed possible. Their lives seemed to get better with each day that passed. During the five years since Leo's birth—and the two before that—her marriage had blown all her expectations out of the water, as had the man with whom she had recently retaken her wedding vows.

Had coming so close to losing each other made them value the love they shared more fiercely? She wasn't sure. But that was the way it was. Giacomo had been by her side throughout her pregnancy with Leo, when she'd been scared of having another miscarriage, though trying very hard not to show it. She remembered the intense brightness in his eyes when she'd safely delivered their baby, and the way he had tenderly cradled his son afterwards.

He had vowed to be a hands-on father and—true to his word—had called a halt to most of his international working trips. These days he delegated. And

Paolo, his aide, was delighted. In a quiet moment he had told Louise she was the best thing which had ever happened to Giacomo, and he was glad that his boss had seen sense at last!

These days the Volterra family spent most of their time in either England or Italy and, with a determined amount of practice and homework, Louise's Italian was almost fluent. And that was important to her. She never wanted to feel like an outsider in the birthplace of her sons and her husband.

They had sold the penthouse Milanese apartment and bought a family home a short distance away from the city centre, with a garden big enough to cope with their growing brood. Summers they spent in the house on the Amalfi coast and Christmas—always—at Barton. In fact, it was there that Louise had invented her own take on the Italian Christmas classic panettone and had given it to one of her Milanese friends to try. Her good friend Maura had loved it and so had her large and extended family. Giacomo had introduced her to someone he knew who owned a food-manufacturing factory and before Louise knew it, the sweet bread had gone into production. This year, sales of Mamma's Mincemeat Panettone had gone through the roof and Louise was being asked if she was interested in extending the line, to embrace a daring fusion of Italian and English cooking.

She looked up to see Giacomo and Leo trudging

through the snow towards the house and heard them chattering away in Italian as she opened the cupboard to reach up for some marshmallows.

'Here. Let me,' said his voice behind her.

'You're so tall,' she purred to her husband, aware that sometimes she sounded like a teenager in the first heady flush of love, rather than a thirty-year-old mother with a third child on the way.

'And you should be taking things more carefully,' Giacomo said sternly as he handed her the packet.

'Mamma, Mamma!' A dark whirlwind of a child hurled himself across the kitchen, wrapping his arms around her hips and placing his head on her swollen belly. 'Can we go and sing carols now?'

'Soon. We have to wait until Aunt Maeve gets here. Why don't you go and get ready and then we'll have some hot chocolate?'

'*Sì*, Mamma!'

She watched as Leo scampered from the kitchen and then looked up to see the expression of love and pride glinting from her husband's eyes.

'Happy?' he questioned.

'So happy. I can't tell you. Even Aunt Maeve seems to have been completely won over by our gorgeous sons. I can't believe she's coming—and that she actually seems to be looking forward to Christmas for the first time in her life!'

'She's family, *mi amore*. And we must all protect

one another and stay close.' For a moment he traced his finger over the taut drum of her belly before lifting her chin with the tips of his fingers, his voice as smoky as his eyes. 'I cannot wait until we are alone together,' he said huskily. 'Because I want to make love to you very, very slowly. But in the meantime, this will have to do.'

He lowered his mouth onto hers and kissed her so long and so sweetly that Louise had to cling on to his broad shoulders, because she honestly thought she might melt into a puddle on the floor.

Eventually she opened her eyes and, side by side, they stared out of the ancient mullioned window of their English home.

'Oh, look,' Giacomo said softly, with nothing but satisfaction in his voice. 'It's snowing again.'

* * * * *

If you lost yourself in
Confessions of His Christmas Housekeeper,
make sure you check out these other
Sharon Kendrick stories!

Cinderella in the Sicilian's World
The Sheikh's Royal Announcement
Cinderella's Christmas Secret
One Night Before the Royal Wedding
Secrets of Cinderella's Awakening

Available now!

#3961 CROWNED FOR HIS CHRISTMAS BABY
Pregnant Princesses
by Maisey Yates

After being swept up in Prince Vincenzo's revenge plans, Eloise is carrying his surprise heir. And the man who vowed never to marry is claiming her—as his royal Christmas bride!

#3962 THE GREEK SECRET SHE CARRIES
The Diamond Inheritance
by Pippa Roscoe

Months after their passionate fling, rumors bring enigmatic Theron to Summer's doorstep—to discover a pregnancy as obvious as the still-sizzling desire between them! He will give their child the family unit he lost. But Summer's trust isn't so easily won...

#3963 DESERT KING'S SURPRISE LOVE-CHILD
by Cathy Williams

When King Abbas was forced to assume the role of ruler, he was forced to walk away from Georgie. Chance reunites them, and he learns two things: she's still utterly enchanting and *he's* a father!

#3964 THE CHRISTMAS SHE MARRIED THE PLAYBOY
Christmas with a Billionaire
by Louise Fuller

To save her pristine image from scandal, Santina must marry notorious playboy Louis. But after a past betrayal, it's not gossip she fears...it's the burning attraction that will make resisting her convenient husband impossible.

#3965 A CONTRACT FOR HIS RUNAWAY BRIDE
The Scandalous Campbell Sisters
by Melanie Milburne

Elodie needs billion-dollar backing to make a success of her fashion brand. As if pitching to a billionaire wasn't hard enough, Lincoln Lancaster is her ex-fiancé! He'll help her, but his deal has one condition: she'll finally meet him at the altar...

#3966 RECLAIMED FOR HIS ROYAL BED
by Maya Blake

Having tracked Delphine down, King Lucca can finally lay his family's scandalous past to rest...if she agrees to play the golden couple in public. And once again set alight by his touch, will Delphine reveal the explosive reason why she left?

#3967 THE INNOCENT'S PROTECTOR IN PARADISE
by Annie West

Tycoon Niall is the only person Lola can turn to when her life is threatened. He immediately offers her a hiding place—his private Gold Coast retreat! He's utterly off-limits, but their fierce desire incinerates any resistance...

#3968 THE BILLIONAIRE WITHOUT RULES
Lost Sons of Argentina
by Lucy King

Billionaire Max plays by his own rules, but there's one person that stands between him and the truth of his birth: tantalizingly tenacious private investigator Alex. And she's demanding they do things her way!

YOU CAN FIND MORE INFORMATION ON UPCOMING HARLEQUIN TITLES, FREE EXCERPTS AND MORE AT HARLEQUIN.COM.

HPCNMRB1121

"Could you give me an update on when Mr. Smith will be available?"

The receptionist's answering smile was polite but formal. "I apologize for the delay. He'll be with you shortly."

"Look, my appointment was—"

"I understand, Ms Campbell. But he's a very busy man. He's made a special gap in his schedule for you. He's not usually so accommodating. You must've made a big impression on him."

"I haven't even met him. All I know is I was instructed to be here close to thirty minutes ago for a meeting with a Mr. Smith to discuss finance. I've been given no other details."

The receptionist glanced at the intercom console, where a small green light was flashing. She looked up again at Elodie with the same polite smile. "Thank you for being so patient. Mr....erm... Smith will see you now. Please go through. It's the third door on the right. The corner office."

The corner office boded well—that meant he was the head honcho. The big bucks began and stopped with him. Elodie came to the door and took a deep, calming breath, but it did nothing to settle the frenzy of switchblades in her stomach. She gave the door a quick rap with her knuckles. *Please, please, please let me be successful this time.*

"Come."

Her hand paused on the doorknob, her mind whirling in ice-cold panic. Something about the deep timbre of that voice sent a shiver scuttling over her scalp like a small claw-footed creature. How could this Mr. Smith sound so like her ex-fiancé? Scarily alike. She turned the doorknob and pushed the door open, her gaze immediately fixing on the tall dark-haired man behind the large desk.

"You?" Elodie gasped, heat flooding into her cheeks and other places in her body she didn't want to think about right now.

Lincoln Lancaster rose from his chair with leonine grace, his expression set in its customary cynical lines—the arch of one ink-black brow over his intelligent blue-green gaze, the tilt of his sensual mouth that was not quite a smile. His black hair was brushed back from his high forehead in loose waves that looked like they had last been combed by his fingers. He was dressed in a three-piece suit that hugged his athletic frame, emphasizing the broadness of his shoulders, the taut trimness of his chest, flat abdomen and lean hips. He was the epitome of successful a man in his prime. Potent, powerful, persuasive. He got what he wanted, when he wanted, how he wanted.

"You're looking good, Elodie." His voice rolled over her as smoothly and lazily as his gaze, the deep, sexy rumble so familiar it brought up a host of memories she had fought for seven years to erase. Memories in her flesh that were triggered by being in his presence. Erotic memories that made her hyperaware of his every breath, his every glance, his every movement.

Don't miss
A Contract for His Runaway Bride,
available December 2021 wherever
Harlequin Presents books and ebooks are sold.

Harlequin.com

HPEXP1121

et 4 FREE REWARDS!

We'll send you 2 FREE Books plus 2 FREE Mystery Gifts.

PRESENTS
The Flaw in His
Red-Hot Revenge
ABBY GREEN

Harlequin Presents books feature the glamorous lives of royals and billionaires in a world of exotic locations, where passion knows no bounds.

FREE
Value Over
$20

YES! Please send me 2 FREE Harlequin Presents novels and my 2 FREE gifts (gifts are worth about $10 retail). After receiving them, if I don't wish to receive any more books, I can return the shipping statement marked "cancel." If I don't cancel, I will receive 6 brand-new novels every month and be billed just $4.55 each for the regular-print edition or $5.80 each for the larger-print edition in the U.S., or $5.49 each for the regular-print edition or $5.99 each for the larger-print edition in Canada. That's a savings of at least 11% off the cover price! It's quite a bargain! Shipping and handling is just 50¢ per book in the U.S. and $1.25 per book in Canada.* I understand that accepting the 2 free books and gifts places me under no obligation to buy anything. I can always return a shipment and cancel at any time. The free books and gifts are mine to keep no matter what I decide.

Choose one: ☐ **Harlequin Presents**
Regular-Print
(106/306 HDN GNWY)

☐ **Harlequin Presents**
Larger-Print
(176/376 HDN GNWY)

Name (please print)

Address   Apt. #

City   State/Province   Zip/Postal Code

Email: Please check this box ☐ if you would like to receive newsletters and promotional emails from Harlequin Enterprises ULC and its affiliates. You can unsubscribe anytime.

Mail to the **Harlequin Reader Service:**
IN U.S.A.: P.O. Box 1341, Buffalo, NY 14240-8531
IN CANADA: P.O. Box 603, Fort Erie, Ontario L2A 5X3

Want to try 2 free books from another series? Call 1-800-873-8635 or visit www.ReaderService.com.

*Terms and prices subject to change without notice. Prices do not include sales taxes, which will be charged (if applicable) based on your state or country of residence. Canadian residents will be charged applicable taxes. Offer not valid in Quebec. This offer is limited to one order per household. Books received may not be as shown. Not valid for current subscribers to Harlequin Presents books. All orders subject to approval. Credit or debit balances in a customer's account(s) may be offset by any other outstanding balance owed by or to the customer. Please allow 4 to 6 weeks for delivery. Offer available while quantities last.

Your Privacy—Your information is being collected by Harlequin Enterprises ULC, operating as Harlequin Reader Service. For a complete summary of the information we collect, how we use this information and to whom it is disclosed, please visit our privacy notice located at corporate.harlequin.com/privacy-notice. From time to time we may also exchange your personal information with reputable third parties. If you wish to opt out of this sharing of your personal information, please visit readerservice.com/consumerschoice or call 1-800-873-8635. **Notice to California Residents**—Under California law, you have specific rights to control and access your data. For more information on these rights and how to exercise them, visit corporate.harlequin.com/california-privacy.

HP21R2

Love Harlequin roman

DISCOVER.

Be the first to find out about promotions, news and exclusive content!

f Facebook.com/HarlequinBooks

🐦 Twitter.com/HarlequinBooks

📷 Instagram.com/HarlequinBooks

📌 Pinterest.com/HarlequinBooks

You Tube YouTube.com/HarlequinBooks

ReaderService.com

EXPLORE.

Sign up for the Harlequin e-newsletter and download a free book from any series at **TryHarlequin.com**

CONNECT.

Join our Harlequin community to share your thoughts and connect with other romance readers!
Facebook.com/groups/HarlequinConnection

◆ **HARLEQUIN**

HSOCIAL2021